BORROWED TIME

LEAH R CUTTER

KNOTTED ROAD PRESS

The Fairy-Bridge Troll

The Troll-Demon War

The Troll-Human War

The Troll-Troll War

The Shadow Wars Trilogy

The Raven and the Dancing Tiger

The Guardian Hound

War Among the Crocodiles

The Clockwork Fairy Kingdom

The Clockwork Fairy Kingdom

The Maker, the Teacher, and the Monster

The Dwarven Wars

The Chronicles of Franklin

Franklin Versus The Popcorn Thief

Franklin Versus The Soul Thief

Franklin Versus The Child Thief

Huli Intergalactic - Science/Space Fantasy

Origins

The Strawberry Girl

Contemporary Fantasy

Siren's Call

The Immortals' War

CONTENTS

LIFE ONE

LIFE TWO

LIFE THREE

LIFE FOUR

LIFE FIVE

LIFE SIX

LIFE SEVEN

LIFE EIGHT

LIFE NINE

LIFE TEN?

LIFE ONE

Merilee woke with a start from her nightmare of endless water and drowning, drawing a gasping breath.

Sweet air—not water—filled her lungs.

She sucked in great gulps, trying to calm her racing heart. She clutched her warm, flannel sheets around her, trying to stop her shivering. She was almost thirty—far too old for nightmares anymore. Beyond her ragged breathing, the night surrounding her was quiet, not even cars sounding in the streets of her sleepy neighborhood.

Merilee tried to focus her thoughts away from her overwhelming fear and to consider her situation. While she wasn't a Seer, she *was* still a witch. Admittedly, she didn't have a lot of magical power, and what she did have came grudgingly.

However, having the same nightmare—drowning in deep, cold water—for the last three nights in a row *had* to mean something.

But what?

Merilee didn't live by the ocean, she lived in land-locked

Minnesota. And not beside any of the Great Lakes or even in the Twin Cities, no, she was down south, here in Rochester. There were some artificial lakes nearby, as well as the Zumbro River. However, she never went boating or fishing. There wasn't any reason for her to get close to the water, and now, with these dreams, she had no intention of going anywhere near it.

Plus, the water in her nightmares had always seemed vast. Much bigger than a lake. Endless miles deep.

Maybe she should call her cousin Natalie, who was a Seer, and who could not only tell you that you'd break your toe in the next year but how you'd have your eggs the following Tuesday. However, Natalie refused to ever tell anyone their future over the phone. Plus, she lived in Seattle, which was near the water.

Merilee shook her head, then sighed. No, she was going to have to talk with her big sister Angelina, who would probably look on Merilee's nightmares as yet *another* personal failing.

But Angelina was one of the most powerful witches Merilee knew—strong enough to generate thunderstorms when she got really mad.

Not that Merilee resented her sister's easy access to magic. Much.

Merilee shivered again, sitting up in her bed, reassuring herself that all was well. A sliver of light from the streetlight in the alley outside slid through the gap in the curtains to her left. Past the foot of her bed stood an ancient wooden bureau. On top of it was her metal jewelry stand full of dangling earrings and necklaces, a beautiful porcelain bowl holding her bracelets, and a cute fetish-toad carved out of sandstone that had been a souvenir of her visit to New Mexico.

To the left of her bureau was her closet door, firmly shut.

It wasn't that she believed monsters could come through it—Angelina had made sure that Merilee's house was too well guarded for some stray portal to manifest inside. Still, it always made her feel better to sleep with the closet door shut.

To the right of the bureau was the door leading to the rest of the second floor of Merilee's house, which stayed open. She only ever closed that door when she had visitors staying with her. It didn't even have a lock on it. On the adjoining wall stood the door to her bathroom, also firmly shut.

Merilee shook her head. Everything looked and felt fine. She didn't smell smoke, just the remains of the trout she'd fried in lemon and butter for dinner.

Then she glanced at the glowing red numbers of her alarm clock, sitting on the white end table to the right of her bed.

1:23 AM.

1-2-3.

An inauspicious time to wake up from a nightmare.

1-2-3. Go?

A loud *thunk* came from downstairs.

What the hell was that?

Merilee slid from her bed as silently as she could. She tiptoed to the door of her bedroom, then paused on the threshold and listened.

"Would you watch it?" came whispered words.

"Sorry, boss," came a second voice.

A third voice piped up. "Sorry."

Shit. Three men downstairs. (Merilee didn't question that they were men—it was just something she sensed.)

What did they want? Were they here to rob her? Or worse? She wasn't wearing any clothes. She'd locked her front door, hadn't she? She'd never bothered setting up too many physical barriers for her home. She'd always concentrated on the magical ones, as her sister had instructed her to, carefully following the written-out instructions for how to "arm" her house.

It wasn't as though Merilee anticipated any magical attacks. She didn't have that much power. No one would ever think of her as a threat.

Unlike her older sister.

"Come on," Merilee heard the boss whisper. "Let's get her."

Shit. They *were* coming for her.

Why? She knew it wasn't for anything she'd done. It must be because of Angelina. What the hell had Angelina done now? Who had she pissed off?

Merilee glanced quickly around the room. She couldn't set up a portal and transport herself somewhere else. That would take a lot of power and time, as well as ingredients that she didn't have at hand. She couldn't fly out of the window—even the strongest of witches didn't have that capability, no matter what the myths and popular TV shows said. She didn't have the strength to hide herself in a shadow. Any bright light would dispel that illusion immediately.

Hell, she couldn't even hide in her bathroom. She had never put a lock on that door either.

This was her house. She was supposed to be safe here.

But she had to hide. Or, escape. Something. And quickly.

She heard steps on the spiral staircase.

Automatically, she closed her bedroom door, not because it would stop anyone, but to at least to slow the men down.

Merilee's brain froze. What could she do?

She looked wildly around her bedroom.

Transform! Yes! The one spell that usually didn't fail her!

Merilee stepped away from the door, going to the foot of her bed. A transformation spell took power, but not much time. Plus, it needed only a single ingredient: something from the creature she intended to become.

She didn't have any feathers in her bedroom, so she couldn't turn into a bird. No wolf's teeth or bear claws, either.

What she did have was a plush, stuffed cat that always sat on the chest at the foot of her bed. It had soft gray fur, green eyes, and the tip of a pink tongue just sticking out of its white snout. It had been a present from one of her numerous cousins, a joke gift with a teasing note about the toy being the easiest familiar she'd ever find.

Despite the stinging realization that Merilee wasn't strong enough to draw a familiar to her, she still kept the cat.

It would have to do.

Merilee wrapped both her hands around the soft plush toy and urgently whispered the spell. The cat shrank, making her lose her grip for a moment. She stuttered, then continued.

Had she just messed up the spell?

A dark cloud sprang up around her. She blinked, but couldn't see anything. She didn't remember that ever happening before. She continued the spell anyway. She folded in on herself, compressing herself downward, inward.

The men gathered outside her door as Merilee found herself reaching down, her hands, no, paws, now touching the braided rug at the foot of her bed.

Lights came on, blinding her.

She yowled angrily at them.

"What the hell?"

The men had rushed into the room, finding only an empty bed and a very pissed-off cat.

They didn't appear to notice the empty plush animal that had once been a stuffed toy also crumpled on the floor.

Merilee crouched down, growling low in her throat. She glanced over her shoulder.

Huh. Long white hair? She flexed a paw. And six toes. Weird. The plush toy had been covered in gray fur. She'd assumed that she'd just take on its form.

"Where she'd go?" fumed the one who Merilee assumed was the boss.

Thing One replied, "Probably just flew away."

"Damn it!" the boss said. "I told you we needed to be *silent* when we broke in here."

"Think she's gone to warn her sister?" Thing Two asked.

"Probably," the boss replied. "Come on. Let's see if there's anything worth taking."

"What about the cat?" Thing One asked. "Probably her familiar. Look at those green eyes."

Merilee found herself bristling, the fur all along the back of her shoulders rising as the three men stared at her. In her human form she'd had plain brown eyes, along with olive-toned skin.

"We ain't equipped to take her," boss replied. "Probably scratch your face off if you grabbed at her."

Merilee hissed at them, just because she could. Then she scampered past them, running so fast down the spiral staircase that she felt slightly dizzy when she reached the bottom. She had to hide, at least until they were gone.

"That answers that," she heard the boss say behind her. "That cat's a familiar. No doubt about it."

Everything looked so big down here! The comfy chair at the foot of the stairs loomed over her. The end table, covered with her latest jigsaw puzzle, was twice her height.

Then all the scents came swirling in, overwhelming her: the wood fire she'd had in the fireplace at the end of the room, though that had been more than a month ago. The earthy chocolate she'd gotten for herself as a treat last week—

maybe there were still crumbs there? Plus she could smell the strange men in her place, their scents so out of place with everything.

She shook her head. She needed to focus!

Where could she hide? Not under the big purple sofa that rested against the front windows. Though it was huge, the legs were too squat, and it sat too low. Behind it, however…

Merilee dashed around the back of the sofa.

Dust bunnies assailed her. She really was going to have to find a stronger cleaning spell. She stepped past the biggest of them, then delicately sat, her tail wrapping itself automatically around her front paws. She'd placed herself about the center of the couch, too far in for anyone to grab her from a side.

And waited.

She licked her chest.

Ugh. Gross.

But it felt so soothing, so she found herself doing it again.

It actually wasn't that bad. Besides, how else was she supposed to clean herself?

Eventually, the men tromped down the stairs and out the door. They opened and closed it several times. What were they doing? Were they letting others in? Or were they carting her stuff away? What were they taking? Probably all her magical ingredients. Some of those were actually quite expensive.

Merilee bristled, but remained quiet. The smell of the cool night outside tickled her nose.

Finally, silence reigned through the house.

Merilee sagged with relief. Oh, thank the Goddess, they were gone.

She still made herself wait for what felt like an endless

amount of time but was probably less than five minutes before she snuck around the edge of the couch.

Damn it! They'd fooled her! Thing One crouched just past the corner of the couch with a large widespread bag in his hands, ready to grab her.

Idiots had left the door open, though.

Merilee streaked past the man. He wasn't quick enough to even touch her fur.

She fled out into the night.

Dew-soaked grass wet her paws. She was so glad it was May and not December! Many scents struck her again, like fresh dirt, hard concrete, spilled beer down the gutter, the nearby lilacs and pines. The bright flash of brakes on a passing car startled her, the gravel she bounded across bruising her paws.

In mere seconds she hid again, under the rose bushes of Mrs. Murphy, across the street.

She heard the men curse at each other. She found herself laughing, a weird bobbing of her head expressing the emotion.

Huh. She hadn't realized cats laughed.

Merilee waited until the men had left, then raced back across the street and into her own backyard.

She wasn't sure how she'd be able to get back into her house. Maybe the men had left the front door unlocked. She couldn't reach the doorhandle in her current form, but that didn't matter.

Merilee found she couldn't say the words to the transformation spell out loud. She did vocalize, though, sounding like a cat in heat. She tried to stay quiet, but couldn't really keep her voice down.

Hopefully she wouldn't wake any of her neighbors.

However, when she finished the spell, nothing changed. She remained a white cat, crouched down in her backyard, the concrete patio blocks cold under her four paws as well as her butt.

She tried again, this time, not caring how loud she was. She felt the urge to move, to pace, but she made herself sit still.

Nothing happened.

Not even a glimmer of magic passed by her.

Merilee had done transformation spells before. Merely the act of thinking and vocalizing the spell should have brought her back to her normal state. What was going wrong this time? Did she have to be able to say the words out loud? Human-type words? But how could she? She had a cat mouth. She couldn't articulate such syllables. Maybe she needed a vocalization spell? She would need ingredients for that!

As well as opposable thumbs.

One last time, Merilee tried to reverse the transformation spell, this time, pacing counterclockwise in a tight circle.

It felt much better to move while doing magic. Was that why she'd always had such a tough time with magic, as her mother and sister always stood stock still when they cast a spell? She'd have to remember that, and try walking, or at the very least, swaying when she did magic.

Wind rustled her fur as she paced and yowled, sending chills down her spine and shooting her tail straight out behind her.

At least she caught a whiff of magic this time, smelling like lavender butter cake.

But she didn't change in the least; no transformation overtook her.

She sat down again, finding herself automatically grooming her long fur.

Now what?

She sighed, a short, expressive cat-sigh.

She'd planned on contacting Angelina first thing in the morning anyway. She had to warn her sister about the robbers.

Might as well just show up on her doorstep.

Hopefully her big sister wouldn't laugh too hard when she saw her.

CHAPTER 2

Merilee paused by the side of the street, panting. She resisted the urge to sprawl across the warm blacktop. She'd just muss up her fur, again, and have to pause to groom herself. Again.

The day had dawned with a clear blue sky and an overly hot sun. During the night, she'd been grateful for her long hair. Now, it was far too hot. White fur wasn't the best color either. It kept getting dirty.

Cicadas buzzed in the tall grass that rustled beside her. Butterflies flitted above her head. She'd had to fight the urge to pounce and chase after them.

At least she wasn't hungry—she'd killed the mouse before she'd been able to stop herself. The warm blood had soothed her throat, and the taste, well, it hadn't tasted like chicken, not exactly, but close enough.

However, she was still miles and *miles* away from Angelina's house, though Merilee had walked most of the morning.

Try as hard as she could, Merilee just couldn't make her

little legs go any faster. Sure, a cat could sprint really fast, particularly when someone was coming after them.

They just weren't made for traveling long distances.

Merilee had never walked to her sister's house. Like every right-thinking person, she drove everywhere.

Besides, Angelina lived on the other side of Rochester, to the north, in one of the nicer neighborhoods. Not quite a gated community, but close. While Merilee lived closer to the railroad, on the poorer side of town.

Angelina worked as a paralegal, while Merilee just drove a school bus.

No one would hire her now. Not while she was a cat. What would she do if she couldn't change back?

Merilee didn't want to admit to herself how much she felt, well, at home, as a cat. It just seemed to suit her better.

However, she didn't want to live as someone's pet. She wanted her freedom. She shivered despite the heat.

She needed shade. And water. And her human legs, damn it!

She heard a car approaching from behind. She slipped off the side of the road, hiding in the tall grass.

She didn't know if the robbers who'd come to her house earlier were still searching for her. She had to assume they were, however.

A long-haired white cat making its way down the road was just too easy, and obvious, of a target. Plus, Rochester wasn't that big of a town, not really. And there weren't that many ways to get to her sister's house.

Merilee paused, sitting her butt down on the cool earth and bringing up one paw. She immediately licked it and wiped her face with it before she could stop herself.

The pads of her paw had been pink earlier, before she'd spent the morning walking dusty roads. She stopped herself from licking it clean. Barely.

It took some thought to figure out how to flex her paw and bring her claws out. She assumed it would happen automatically if she was fighting someone.

Sharp, hooked talons came out from all six toes, plus the one up her leg—a dewclaw? Was that what it was called?

They sure looked deadly. She almost wished she'd let the robbers get closer to her, just so she could have sliced one of them open.

The fur along her front leg went all the way down and covered the top of her paw. Was she a Persian? She assumed so, given the mass of fur.

The car that she'd heard coming down the road slowed, then pulled to a stop. The doors opened.

"Here, kitty kitty," she heard.

"Shut up, you!"

That was the robbers. And the boss.

Damn it! They were still after her.

How could she hide? She needed shadows. Something to blend into.

Shadow. Darkness. Shade. Coolness.
Black.

The words rang through her head. She found herself pacing again, a close, tight circle.

Black. Dark. Gloom. Shadow.

A shiver washed over her. Darkness stole her sight. A shiver raised the hair along her spine and bushed out her tail.

The words looped around again. She found herself sitting.

The loud sound of footsteps though the tall grass drew nearer.

Merilee remained rooted to the spot. Magic sprang up around her, a pixie curtain smelling of fresh cedar and sweet strawberries.

She'd slice those men to pieces if they grabbed for her.

The darkness dissolved. Bright sunlight shone down on her head again, heating up the space between her wide perked ears.

She tensed, ready to fight or flee if they came after her again.

The sound of steps stopped. She looked up at them, expecting sudden harsh hands grabbing her.

"I told you that wasn't her!" said the boss.

They tromped back to the car. It moved away.

Merilee blinked. What had just happened?

Then she looked down.

She no longer had white fur. Instead, she was black as coal. Short haired, finally.

Huh. How had she done that? It hadn't felt like a human spell.

Maybe it was a cat spell. Could cats do magic?

Did she have to learn a whole different set of magical incantations and rules?

She sighed. Angelina had always accused Merilee of being lazy, telling her more than once that she had power and just needed to apply herself more.

But Merilee found magic, well, boring. All those long lists of ingredients to memorize. And spells. And incantations. And…

Did cats not have to memorize spells? Or at least, not like humans? Did magic come more naturally to them?

What else could she instinctively do as a cat?

For the first time in what felt like forever, Merilee felt excited about magic, like she had when she'd been a teenager and just coming into her power. There had to be things she could do. She just had to figure out what.

CHAPTER 3

Cats regularly appeared out of nowhere, tripping their owners up. Though Merilee had never owned a cat, she did know that much, from watching other people and their animals. Plus, she'd seen more than one comic strip about such things.

It didn't take Merilee long to figure out how to generate a cat-portal and to transport herself. She'd needed focus and pacing, but no yowling, to make a small, cat-sized oval of blue light appear.

The first few times she hadn't been able to transport herself very far. First it was just across a yard, then from one end of the block to the other. Gradually she'd increased the distance, until this last hop had been half a mile at least, and she stepped through the portal into Angelina's backyard.

The sun was just starting to set. Merilee considered changing back into a long-furred cat again, but she knew Angelina would bitch about the hair on her pristine furniture.

Maybe Merilee should do it out of spite…

Angelina had an impressive backyard, much larger than Merilee's. Her house sat on half an acre, at the foot of a hill. The backyard had three tiers, the middle one being the "fairy garden," the area lined with a circle of blessed rocks, so Merilee, Angelina, and the other local witches could dance the entire night of the summer solstice. The top tier had a small fountain that even this early in the year had cheery water splashing.

Merilee went to the back door, sitting down on the rough mat that tickled her paws.

She couldn't open the door. Couldn't even reach the doorbell. Maybe if she leaped up, she could, but that felt, well, humiliating. She couldn't transport herself into the house either: she felt the pressure of Angelina's magical protections gently pushing her away. They rubbed her fur the wrong way, though she wasn't exactly sure why.

Maybe she would have to try to reach the doorbell, though, if she couldn't find some other way in.

Merilee walked along the small concrete sidewalk that curved around the side of the house, heading for the front yard. Perhaps she could find a better way into the house from the front—an open window or something.

And stopped.

Huge boxwoods grew in the front of Angelina's house. She kept them well trimmed into square hedges.

The robbers crouched behind them on either side of Angelina's front door. They were dressed all in black, now, like amateur ninjas.

They'd nab her sister when she came out, unsuspecting.

Merilee found the back of her neck automatically bristling, the hair rising up. A low growl sounded deep in her throat.

However, she was only a cat. She couldn't attack them.

She had to scare the robbers away. Save her sister, somehow.

Save the day, despite her current size and stature.

She was sure she could do it.

But how?

CHAPTER 4

Merilee paced around the fairy garden three times before coming up with a plan.

First, she changed her fur again, turning herself back into a bright-white, long-haired Persian. Why she could change the color of her fur and not transform back into a human puzzled her. Something must really have gone wrong with the first transformation spell.

It wasn't twilight, not yet, but clouds had filled the sky and darkness was coming soon. The smell of rain floated through the air, along with scents of fresh grass and lilacs.

When Merilee was ready, she raced up to the front of the house, yowled once, twice, hissed, then raced to the back yard again, still yowling.

The robbers knew they'd been found.

As she'd hoped, they left their hiding places to chase after her.

Merilee didn't know if she'd made enough noise that Angelina might glance out her window, or even better, step into her backyard, looking for who was causing such trouble.

At least Angelina would be prepared, as opposed to innocently walking out her door and into an ambush.

The men chased Merilee down the concrete sidewalk and into the back yard. She knew she had no place to hide here. Angelina kept the grass cut short. The bushes on the edges of the yard were also well trimmed. While Merilee could go underneath them, she couldn't hide.

Perhaps she could go over the fence, though she judged it as too high to easily jump over.

The three robbers stopped once they reached the bottom tier of the yard and looked around.

Really? They were just going to give up? Not chase her anymore? Geez.

Merilee raced toward them again, yowling, as if she was a huge creature challenge them, forcing them away from her territory.

Because really, it felt that way. This space was *hers*. It belonged to her family. Who were these men intruding on her property?

The men backed up. Merilee didn't stop hissing or yowling, despite how scared at least one of the Things looked. She focused on him.

He took a step back. Then another.

Good. She would drive him away first, then deal with the others.

Crap.

The others.

Merilee saw a flash out of the corner of her eye but it was too late. Even her speedy cat reflexes weren't quick enough.

The other Thing captured her in a rough burlap sack.

Merilee hissed and yowled. She hooked the cloth with her claws and tried to tear it.

She felt herself flying through the air, only to land with a solid *thunk*.

She cried out, dazed.

Had one of the robbers just swung the bag and hit it against the side of the house?

She crouched lower when she felt the air whizzing through the loose-woven burlap again.

This time, she hit her head.

Dazed, Merilee shook herself. Then she stopped moving. Stopped making noise.

"Think that killed her?" Thing One asked.

"Takes more than that to kill a familiar," the boss replied. "Come on. I got an idea."

Merilee shivered. Where were they taking her? What were they going to do to her? And how could she get out of this mess?

CHAPTER 5

Whichever Thing had the bag whacked it one last time, probably against the door of the car. Merilee was certain her entire side was one solid bruise. The bag had little air or light. She found herself panting in the darkness.

Where were they taking her?

Though she hurt, she could easily push away her pain, ignore it. Huh. She'd never been able to do that as a human. Was that another cat thing?

She closed her eyes. She'd tear her way out of the bag as soon as they left her somewhere.

To her surprise, she found that she slept. Quite comfortably, actually.

She only woke when someone picked up the bag again. She complained, loudly.

And regretted it an instant later when she was whacked against the hood of the car.

She shook her head, feeling lightheaded and dizzy. Where were they? Somewhere outdoors. Cold night wind blew through the rough burlap.

She smelled fish.

And water.

Before she could voice her displeasure once more, she found herself flying through the air. The time seemed endless.

Then she hit the water.

Cold. Dark. Wet.

Merilee froze.

Just like in her nightmares.

Frantically, Merilee scratched at the bag. She couldn't see anything, but she felt herself making progress. She tore a small hole in the bag, followed by a larger tear.

She couldn't breathe.

She drifted down into the bottomless lake. No current to take her away.

She was going to die. She couldn't swim. She couldn't even float, not with her heavy fur dragging her down.

She tore at the bag, finally freeing herself.

She needed to create a portal. Something. Now.

She waved her paws, churning them rapidly in the water. Her lungs ached with the lack of air. The cold wrapped firmly around her, freezing her limbs, slowing her down. It smelled of rotten seaweed—lake weed—and death.

A small oval of light appeared to her left.

That didn't look right. It wasn't similar to the cat portals she'd created before.

Those had been a small circle of blue light.

This was gray, like lighted clouds, and the center was the blackest night.

Merilee propelled herself toward the oval.

It was a portal, all right.

Not one that she'd created, however.

She reached out one paw.

The portal told her several things.

This was the doorway to the afterlife.

She would lose her life if she went through it.

Or rather, *a* life.

As a cat, she'd only lose *one* of her nine lives. She'd have eight remaining.

As a human, she'd lose the only life she had.

The consequences quickly became clear to her.

If she floated through the portal, she could never go back to being a human.

The portal would take one of her lives. As a human, she only had one to give.

If she remained a cat, she would have eight remaining lives.

Merilee paused briefly, but she didn't really have a choice.

She wanted to live, no matter what form she might take.

She bunched herself together, then pushed out, gliding easily toward the opening. Crossing it felt like passing through a window of ice. Cold instantly pierced her, all the way to her core. Jagged edges combed through her fur, snagging pieces of it and keeping them. It took all her will to push herself forward, through the freezing endless hoop, until she finally reached the far side.

Light surrounded her as she reached the other side, tugging her upward.

No! she tried to scream, twisting around. She felt the pull of the light, lifting her higher.

She knew that she just had to turn her face toward it, and the light would carry her off and away. Out of the darkness.

Was there a cat heaven? She wasn't sure. There was certain to be a blissful resting place.

However, Merilee wanted to live too much. Besides, she had to get back to her sister Angelina, warn her of the stupid thugs who were gunning for her, for both of them.

The light paused, then gave her a solid push.

Suddenly, Merilee felt slimy wet mud under her paws. It

was gross and disgusting and how long would it take to clean her feet *now*? But it was also marvelous and wonderful, filling her with a purr inducing joy.

She was alive. She had lost a life, but she had eight more.

Hopefully she wouldn't need all of them before this was done…

Merilee shook herself. She stood on a dark shore. Full night had come. She was soaking wet, cold, starving, and more than a little angry.

Whoever those men were, they had better watch out now. She might be just a cat, but she was a cat hell bent on vengeance.

LIFE TWO

Merilee paced and growled on the shores of the Zumbro River. She'd changed her form, going from that of a long-haired white cat back to a short-haired black one, so at least her fur was now dry. Her paws were still muddy, but she wasn't going to bother cleaning them until she was out of the wilderness and back into civilization.

All right, so she was actually in a park, not out in the tundra somewhere. It still felt like the middle of nowhere. The would-be cat-assassins had picked a spot on the river that was out of the way. No one was around, or likely to be passing by until morning. The smell of humans that was constantly tickling Merilee's nose had actually faded, and the smells of water reeds, sunbaked pines, and lilacs were carried on the breezes. Plus a hundred other smaller shades of scent, but Merilee didn't have the time or patience to chase them all down at this point.

Instead, she tried desperately to come up with a plan, something that would somehow save her sister. She didn't know if the three thugs had gone back to Angelina's house. Maybe they had gone back to *her* house, seeing if they could find her. Now that they thought they'd hurt her by supposedly killing her familiar.

Merilee had never had a familiar. She'd known from a young age that she probably never would. They only came to certain witches, those who had a taste for the outdoors and wild things. Plus, to entice a familiar to stay with a witch, you had to have a certain level of power. Familiars weren't a one-way street. It wasn't just the witch who gained abilities with a familiar. The animal did as well. It was a voluntary agreement, at least among the witches that Merilee knew and associated with.

Were there witches who just enslaved the poor animal that they intended on using? It wouldn't surprise her. There was a reason why people said to not suffer a witch to live.

Try as she might, Merilee couldn't come up with a decent plan. A big part of her problem was that she had no idea who those men were, why they'd originally set out to kidnap her. Why had they believed that killing her familiar would further their plans? She knew it had nothing to do with her.

This was all Angelina's fault.

There wasn't any way that Merilee could just appear inside Angelina's house. It was too well protected. And she didn't want to take a chance of being captured by the stupid thugs again.

No, Merilee was just going to have to spend the night outdoors, on her own. She wasn't too afraid. It wasn't like she was a human woman sleeping in a park, with the constant fear of drunken men looking to assault her. Instead, her main concerns would be other predators, like raccoons, coyotes, or even large eagles.

Merilee arched her back, stretching each and every vertebra as she did so. Goddess, yoga had *never* felt this good. She ambled slowly over to a tree, then sat at the base of it, looking up.

Would climbing the tree be a good idea? Would she be able to get down again? She'd never been afraid of heights. Actually, the reverse had always been the case. She loved being up high. She remembered her mother accusing her of always seeking the highest point as a child, whenever they went on a walk somewhere, just so she could give her poor mother a heart attack.

Merilee held out one black paw against the dark tree trunk. It looked like a shadow on a shadow. No one would see her up in the limb just there.

Would it be comfortable enough? Could she sleep there? Would she fall out of the tree? She didn't know.

Merilee paused for a moment, closing her eyes and taking a deep breath, encouraging whatever cat-like instincts she had to come forward.

When she opened her eyes again, everything seemed brighter. She could see more of the tree trunk in front of her, the park bench just beyond, and the river flowing silently. It was as if her true night vision had finally kicked in. She squatted down, wriggling her butt naturally to ensure that she had a solid base, then leapt upwards.

Her claws automatically grabbed onto the rough bark. As she pulled herself up, the claws naturally disengaged.

It didn't take long before Merilee found herself in the crook of the first branch. It had a flat enough area as the branch spread out from the trunk. Merilee paused and looked down. She knew that shouldn't jump down from this spot. Even as a cat, she'd possibly hurt something. She was out of easy reach. A human would need to get a ladder or something to fetch her out.

Should she go up farther? She paused and looked above her, through the canopy of large maple leaves. No, the branches quickly grew thinner, until they were merely twigs.

Merilee found herself walking the smallest circle possible,

her feet practically tripping over one another as she moved herself around. Then she went around again, only in the other direction.

Was it just her imagination, or was the branch she was on spreading out slightly?

Merilee pushed her paws out, pressing down near the edges of the flat space.

Yes, the branch was growing larger: primarily wider and flatter.

She took another turn, this time getting in a full two steps. She found herself not purring, not exactly. Making a soft guttural sound would be a better description. Almost like a growling purr.

Finally, she was satisfied. The branch would accommodate her nicely. She had no fear of falling off, now.

With a final few licks of her sides, ensuring that her fur was clean enough, Merilee curled up into a ball, her tail over her nose, and purred herself to sleep.

CHAPTER 7

Merilee still didn't have a good plan when the bright light of the sun woke her. She had no idea what time it was, except that it was time to get up. She didn't bother standing up and stretching, not yet. First she opened one eye, then the other, and looked around, making sure that no one was near.

The park was mostly empty. There were a couple of joggers along the path, heading away from her. No one was watching her. Merilee carefully stood and stretched, arching her back again, then giving a face-splitting yawn.

She could always sleep again later, catch a nap. She might have to. Her new body didn't appear to be built to stay up for hours on end, but to be awake for a while, then to sleep a short time, then be awake again.

Strange. As a human, she'd always longed for the same schedule. During the summer, when she wasn't driving school buses, she'd always fallen into that sort of schedule for herself: waking with the dawn, sleeping for a short time around 10 AM, staying awake until 3ish, then falling asleep again for a longer nap, before getting up one last time for the longest period of time, before falling asleep again around midnight.

Now, how to get down the tree? She knew she couldn't go down head first. She'd fall. Instead, she scrambled around, backing down the tree slowly, always looking over her shoulder, until she could finally leap and land gracefully.

It didn't take her long to catch an unwary bird. She tried not to think about it too hard, how satisfying the kill had been, how soothing the blood and meat were.

After spending possibly far too long cleaning her face and her paws, Merilee set off again. Only this time, she wasn't going to Angelina's house. The thugs might still be there. Hopefully, not surrounding Angelina's door, as they had been the night before.

However, if her sister hadn't gone outside at all last night, the thugs would have left, right? There would be too many people around for them to stay. No, her sister was probably quite safe for the moment, and would be heading to her office soon.

Angelina worked as a paralegal for a group of lawyers in the downtown area. Though their mom had always hoped that Angelina would go back to college, get a law degree, and become a full-time lawyer, Merilee knew that Angelina would never leave where she was. She was, as she said, "the power behind the throne." She adamantly didn't want the headaches the lawyers had, or have to work the hours they did. Though there was occasional overtime, for the most part, Angelina had her nights and weekend free to do the other things she loved, like magic and witchcraft.

It was another reason why Angelina stayed here, in Rochester, Minnesota, instead of moving to the Twin Cities. She'd always preferred being a big fish in a small pond, rather than fighting with the other big fish.

So now, all Merilee had to do was to get herself to

Angelina's office. Then get into the office, somehow. And then convince Angelina that Merilee in this current form was, in fact, her sister.

Was there any magic she could do, so that Angelina would at least see that Merilee wasn't an ordinary cat?

She thought about how she'd been able to change the color of her fur. Maybe she could appear to Angelina as a white cat, then the next moment, as a black cat. That might do it, or at least convince her that Merilee wasn't an ordinary cat.

The whole sister thing would have to come later.

Satisfied that her fur was clean enough for now, Merilee strolled through the park, on her way downtown. She would make herself some portals to shorten the journey.

Once she arrived, she had to scope out the place. Then maybe take a well-earned nap.

CHAPTER 8

Merilee found that she really, *really* didn't like spending all her time walking on concrete. It hurt the pads of her feet! And she had to be careful. Sometimes, her claws would click on the hard material. What was the point of being a silent killer when she wasn't always completely quiet?

At least she'd found a good shadow to hide in, where she could watch all the silly humans walking in and out of Angelina's building. Hiding in shadows was *so* much easier as a cat.

As she'd suspected, doing magic in her cat form came more naturally to Merilee than it ever had in her human form. She'd never enjoyed memorizing spells or lists of ingredients and the order to use them in. There was an old joke among her family that the only way to tell the difference between a chef and a witch was to figure out which one used lizard feet and which one used chicken feet. Chances were the former was the witch, but you could never be sure, particularly in these modern times with odd cuisine.

Hiding in the shadows was merely a matter of pacing a

few times, growling softly, all the hair along her hackles rising up and her tail poofing out.

Then, she could sit calmly in the shade, occasionally licking her fur. She'd even found the opportunity to catch a short nap, as it was still far too early for Angelina to make her appearance.

At least the day was still sunny, though her nose told her that there would be rain by midafternoon. She wasn't looking forward to that at all. Though maybe she could find someplace dry, or use some sort of magic to make it dry enough…

She shook her head, yawning, making herself focus on those walking up the broad steps into the office building. It was an old converted bank, part of historic downtown (though honestly, there weren't that many old buildings. And Merilee *really* didn't see the point in them. Particularly not when her much better nose could smell the mold and decay that was already present in some of that old concrete and wood).

Finally, her patience was rewarded. Angelina was walking up the stairs with a travel mug full of her own special brew of coffee, sugar-free chocolate and hazelnut syrups, soy milk and protein powder.

It made Merilee nauseous thinking about it, and that was *before* she'd turned into a cat.

Angelina wore a white blouse that was too tight. Merilee felt uncomfortable just looking at it. She also wore a black pencil skirt, again, far too restrictive for Merilee.

Had her sister always worn such tight clothing? Who was she trying to impress? Or did she wear it as a distraction? Get the men looking at her chest so that they wouldn't necessarily pay attention to the words coming out of her mouth, until it was far too late?

At least Angelina wore sensible black shoes. Merilee

found herself bobbing her head up and down again, that weird cat equivalent of a laugh.

Angelina was in kitten heels. How appropriate.

Merilee shook herself. A part of her just wanted to do one more deep stretch. Instead, she made herself bound out of the shadows.

Nearby pigeons startled as she leapt past them.

She did note their resting place. One of them might become lunch.

She didn't stop now, though. She raced like a black streak toward her sister, intending to interrupt her before she slipped inside the building.

However, she hadn't counted on her sister's innate magical abilities.

Despite how fast Merilee was moving, how hard she tried to hold herself in a steady line, she couldn't help but swerve at the last minute.

It was as if a five-foot ball of energy surrounded her sister that nothing could penetrate. At least, nothing moving at speed with magical intent.

Angelina coolly glanced over her shoulder as Merilee helplessly raced by.

At least her sister was aware that there was a cat trying to get her attention.

Even if Merilee couldn't get any closer.

CHAPTER 9

Merilee wasn't sure what to do next. How long would Angelina be in the office? Was there a way for Merilee to sneak in? Then what? She knew that Angelina worked on the second floor. Were there stairs? And doors that she'd have to try to open?

Her cat magic was much more about making the natural world fit to her. Not the artificial, human one.

Merilee went back to her shadow, marking it again as a space where she could stay hidden. She kept an eye out for the three thugs, but fortunately, they never showed up.

She napped, ate, cleaned her fur as best she could, napped again, all while waiting for her sister to reappear.

Fortune appeared to smile on her, finally. Around noon, Angelina came back down the stairs of the office building, walking with one of the other women.

This time, Merilee carefully slunk behind them, never getting too close, always sticking to the shadows and keeping herself hidden.

They appeared to be having lunch together at a little local

restaurant. Tables outside had cute umbrellas to keep customers in the shade. The fried food smelled disgusting, though she could tease out the scent of some luscious fish.

Would Angelina choose a table outside? Could Merilee finally get close enough to her?

They appeared to be at least discussing it, talking with a waitress outside. Merilee watched, wishing she was close enough to hear the conversation.

Damn it! They appeared to be going into the restaurant, to sit indoors.

Merilee couldn't help the yowl that erupted when she saw them turn.

Angelina stopped and looked over her shoulder. Merilee felt her hackles rising, all the hair along her small, white body standing, making her appear twice her normal size.

She yowled again, making sure to catch Angelina's eye.

Was that a hint of recognition? No, probably not.

But Angelina did appear to see her this time. She stared directly at Merilee.

A waft of sour smelling magic flowed her way. If she'd been human, she probably wouldn't have smelled it. Wouldn't have even noticed it.

She found her hair bristling further. Was Angelina trying to send her away?

She fought the spell, staying where she was, yowling a third time.

This time, a puzzled look crossed Angelina's face, as if Merilee wasn't doing what the spell had suggested that she do, namely, turning away to avoid that nasty scent.

Angelina stared directly into Merilee's eyes, holding the connection for a few long moments, before she finally nodded.

Relief flooded Merilee. Angelina had just agreed to meet with her. She wasn't certain how she knew that, but she did.

Good.

Now, all she had to do was wait until her sister had finished her lunch. Then…there would be more trials. She just had to be patient, and move one step at a time.

47

CHAPTER 10

I t felt like *forever* before Angelina finally came out of the restaurant. At least she moved within hearing range before she asked her lunch companion if she would like to have some ice cream.

Merilee followed along behind them, occasionally sorting out the various scents that came her way. The artificial scent of Angelina, that didn't quite cover up her natural smell, a scent that Merilee was surprised to realized that she actually recognized, at least at some level. The smell of hot concrete and stinky cars that lay like a fog underneath all the other scents.

Her eyesight wasn't as good as a cat's. Plus, everything always looked so different! She was so low to the ground, now, and much smaller. People seemed huge.

Angelina only turned back once to make sure that Merilee was following them. It took her a few moments to spot Merilee, and then, only after Merilee purposefully stepped away from the shadows.

It was good to know that Merilee wasn't deluding herself

—she really was more difficult to see in cat form, when she chose to be.

Finally, Angelina and her friend stopped at a cart that sold ice cream which was supposedly hand cranked. Merilee would still turn her nose up at it. There were artificial chemicals in it. It didn't smell like cream and sugar.

Angelina and her friend walked off to a low bench that was under a tree, sitting and eating their treats. She came closer now, looking at them from a few feet away.

She had to be careful, though. The stupid humans walking down the sidewalk didn't always notice her. She would be accidentally kicked if she wasn't watchful.

"Whose cat do you suppose that is?" the friend asked Angelina.

"I'm not sure that cat belongs to anyone," Angelina replied after a few moments. "She might be on her own."

"Is she hungry?"

Merilee rolled her eyes. As if she'd deign to eat those yucky chemicals. Couldn't they tell that their ice cream wasn't as "natural" as they'd been led to believe?

"No, Sue, I don't think so," Angelina said after a few moments. "I think she's pissed off."

Merilee nodded. Yes, she was still pretty pissed off about everything.

"Is she someone's familiar?" the friend—Sue—said after a few moments.

Merilee looked more closely at this Sue person. She wasn't a witch. Merilee was certain of it. Why did she ask about familiars? Did she know about witchcraft?

"Maybe," Angelina said, nodding, though she sounded uncertain.

"Oh! Do you think maybe she wants to be *your* familiar?" Sue asked.

Huh? How did Sue know that Angelina was a witch? She

didn't have any power! Merilee realized that she could smell the magic rolling off Angelina, the scent of summer thunderstorms, while there was nothing from Sue.

Angelina shook her head. "No, Sue, and I think that suggestion just pissed her off more."

"Strange," Sue said.

Merilee was just deciding to take a few steps closer to the women when another vaguely familiar scent made her twitch.

What was that? It was a human smell. Something she recognized but didn't.

Merilee turned around in place, taking in her surroundings.

There. Striding purposefully toward Angelina. It was Thing Two, the smallest and possibly most scared of the three thugs. He had a determined scent around him, as if he'd drawn the short straw for this conflict.

Merilee moved quickly, out of the direct sunlight and into the nearest shadow, apparently vanishing. Or at least, she assumed that was what she did when Sue abruptly asked, "Hey, where did that cat go?"

Merilee watched Thing Two approach.

"Angelina Marquez? Got a message for you," Thing Two called out with a show of bravado that was barely skin deep.

Really, she could smell the fear sweat that streamed down his back.

"You better do as you're told. Or not just your sister's familiar is gonna disappear," he warned.

"Who are you and what are you talking about?" Angelina said, her usual anger tinting her words.

Merilee stayed where she was.

"Just ask your sister," Thing Two said before he sauntered off.

While Merilee's sense of smell had gotten better, her

eyesight hadn't. Still, she would bet that if she could peer close enough, she'd see Thing Two shaking as he left.

"What was that all about?" Sue asked.

Merilee came out of hiding, and deliberately sat in front of the women. She hissed at Thing Two's back, loudly, her hackles rising again.

Thing Two glanced over his shoulder and started, almost tripping, before he scurried away.

Good. Put the fear of the cat into him.

Then she turned back to Angelina, who sat with a puzzled expression on her face.

"One thing's for certain, this cat doesn't like that guy any more than we do," she said.

Merilee made her way over to the bench where Angelina and Sue sat. She looked up at them expectantly for a moment, then proceeded to lightly leap up between them.

"Sure, just make yourself at home," Angelina groused.

"Who do you belong to?" Sue said, curious.

Merilee gave a soft growl. She didn't *belong* to anyone. She was her own person. While she might have said that she was her own cat, she was still a *person*.

Were all cats people? Did they consider themselves as such? Was that why they always appeared so self-possessed?

Someday, she'd have to find a normal cat and see if she could ask.

"Huh," was Angelina's reply.

"What was all that talk about Merilee's familiar?" Sue asked. She reached out a hesitant hand for Merilee to sniff.

It didn't surprise Merilee that Sue knew her name, as she appeared to be good enough friends with Angelina that she'd probably heard her talk of her sister.

Merilee could smell the fish tacos the woman had had for lunch, along with the too-sweet tequila drink. Sue wore too much hand cream to get a good sense of the scent of her.

Merilee would say, though, that Sue was on the lighter side of things, not quite an airhead but along those lines. She was older than Merilee would have guessed, the makeup hiding the wrinkles that Merilee's nose told her were there. She wore a peach-colored blouse that went along with her dyed black hair, her eyes a faded hazel.

Merilee only considered stepping onto the woman's white skirt with her dirty paws briefly. She wouldn't actually do anything like that. Not unless Sue actually did something to piss her off.

"Merilee doesn't have a familiar," Angelina said exasperated. "She doesn't have the power." Then she paused. "But you have something to do with Merilee, don't you?"

Merilee turned to look at her sister. She stared solidly into Angelina's steady dark-brown eyes.

I am Merilee

She thought those words as loudly as she could.

Angelina stared back, then suddenly shook her head, breaking the contact, sitting back.

"No," she said. "That can't be."

Merilee put her paw gently onto Angelina's arm. Her claws slid slightly out of their sheathes, not enough to scratch or pierce, but just enough to get her sister's attention.

Reluctantly, Angelina turned back to Merilee, gazing into her eyes again.

I am *Merilee*

"What is it?" Sue asked.

"The cat—she…she claims to be Merilee. But why are you in cat form? Why don't you change back into human form? Have you been trapped? Are you cursed?"

Merilee shook her head. This was going to take some time. Particularly since all Angelina was now focused on was her, and not on Thing Two and the threat he'd issued.

"Mrrow," Merilee said loudly. She looked in the direction that Thing Two had gone, then back to Angelina. Then she did it again, hoping that Angelina would take the hint.

"What, you want to go? Sweetie, I can't. I need to go back to the office for the afternoon. And the office has a strict 'no pets' policy," Angelina said.

Merilee couldn't believe what she was hearing. She was certain that *she* would have dropped everything if Angelina appeared at her door, with need.

"You can't just leave her here alone," Sue said.

Maybe Merilee did have an ally here. She gave a nod of approval.

"Your sister's been turned into a cat. Probably against her will. You're going to have to take care of her this afternoon," Sue continued.

Merilee leaned back in Sue's direction, sliding her body against Sue's arm.

"See? She agrees with me!" Sue said. She put a tentative hand up and stroked along Merilee's back.

By the goddess, that felt good! Even if Sue was hesitant and obviously didn't know the first thing about petting a cat. She had nice nails though, that made up for it. Until they were too much, and Merilee moved away.

"I suppose you're right," Angelina sighed. "I'll get Frank to transcribe Mr. Hendrickson's deposition. And maybe Janice can look over the McGully contracts."

"And I'll cover for you as well," Sue said. "You just have to promise to tell me everything afterward."

Merilee gave a disapproving "Mrrrrow" at that. This was between her and her sister. It was witch business. She didn't want everything aired to a gossipy mundane.

Sue immediately modified her request. "What you can tell me."

Merilee nodded in approval. That was much better.

"Fine," Angelina said. She turned her attention back to Merilee. "I don't suppose I could get you to wait for me in my car or something, could I?"

Merilee bobbed her head in laughter. The gesture was lost on the two humans.

With a heavy kitty sigh, Merilee hopped to the ground. She turned around once, slowly, making sure that no one was watching. Then she looked back at Angelina.

See you at your home. Your home.

The portal formed quickly. Only Angelina gasped—Sue couldn't see a thing. Merilee hopped through it, glad that she'd had an early start, knowing that it would take several such jumps to get her back to Angelina's house.

She came out in a quiet park that she'd stopped by on her way to Angelina's office, then stepped through again and again, making her way to her sister's.

Hopefully, Angelina would actually meet her there quickly, and not get unavoidably detained at work, as usual.

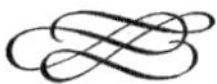

CHAPTER 11

Merilee found she didn't actually mind waiting for her sister that much. She found a nice sunny spot close to the front door, on the immaculately trimmed grass, for a good snooze.

The scents of the two Things and the boss were still present, but fading. They hadn't been back in a while. Hopefully, they wouldn't come back again, though she doubted that was likely to happen.

What exactly did they want from Angelina? Merilee had noticed that hadn't been the part of Thing Two's ultimatum that her sister had focused on. No, she'd zeroed in on the fact that Merilee wasn't strong enough to call a familiar.

Something else was going on, and Merilee intended to discover what it was.

Clouds covering the sun woke her from her nap, not her sister arriving. Great. The wind brought the smell of rain. Merilee wasn't looking forward to getting wet.

Where was Angelina?

Merilee prowled around the front of her sister's house. It was so different, looking at it from her new perspective. She could see where the paint was peeling, down around the edges, where the trim touched the earth. A few brave dandelions had defied Angelina's gardeners, and raised their yellow heads cockily through the boxwoods out front. At least the concrete foundation smelled solid, and the yard smelled green and fresh.

After walking all the way around the house, distracted now and again by bugs or butterflies, Merilee finally heard the familiar engine of Angelina's car. (And funny, how she could identify that sound. As a human, she doubted she would have known it. As a cat, it seemed obvious.)

A large drop of rain plopped down on Merilee's head as she headed toward the front door. She skipped lightly up the steps and waited on the porch while Angelina came up.

"Mrrow," Merilee said, putting as much impatience as she could into the sound.

"I'm sorry, I'm sorry!" Angelina said. "I got held up at the office."

Merilee gave a loud growling sigh, the closest she could give to a "harrumph."

"I said I was sorry," Angelina groused as she unlocked the door, both physically as well as magically. She held the door open with a curious expression.

Merilee walked across the threshold. The spells that Angelina had protecting her house stroked her fur the wrong way. Was that because she was now a cat? Or was it something else?

She'd have to ask Angelina about it later.

She paused just inside the door, looking around. Everything was the same as it had been the last time she'd visited. Well, except for herself.

The great room that the front door opened to was huge. Merilee couldn't see the end of it. Angelina's tasteful black-and-cream-colored leather sofa blocked her view. The floor was spotless, always seen to by one of Angelina's high-powered cleaning spells. Merilee couldn't even smell a dust bunny underneath any of the furniture.

She paused, gathering herself, then leaped up to the back of the sofa, automatically digging her claws in to steady herself.

Oops. Might have just punctured Angelina's couch a little.

"Merilee!" Angelina scolded when she saw the damage. She scooped Merilee up off the couch.

Merilee didn't take kindly to the rough handling. She hissed and scratched at Angelina, who dropped her abruptly.

Merilee landed daintily on her feet, then sat there, looking up calmly at her sister's thunderous expression.

She may have even licked at her paw, then washed her face a little with the side of it.

"You know, I couldn't really believe it when you said that it was you, Merilee," Angelina said, fuming. "Now, I'm pretty sure it is you."

"Mrrow?" Merilee said, expectant. She didn't bother trying to communicate the words, "And now what?" Surely her sister heard them anyway.

"What happened to you?" Angelina said. For the first time, she actually sounded, well, worried. "Are you trapped in that body?"

Merilee held up one paw and tilted it from side to side. Technically, she was trapped as a cat if she wanted to live. She could transform back to a human, but she'd die as soon as she changed.

"Come on," Angelina said, walking through the front room, heading toward the kitchen. "Are you hungry? This might take a while."

"Mrrow," Merilee said, hoping that Angelina took that to be an affirmative. She wasn't starving, but she could eat.

Angelina got out some cooked chicken. Of course, it was skinless. And pretty bland as well, which surprised Merilee. Cooks and witches both knew their way around ingredients. At least it was tender and juicy.

While Merilee crouched on Angelina's kitchen counter and daintily chewed at her chicken, Angelina gathered ingredients for what Merilee assumed was either a vocalization spell for her, or some sort of *speak with animals* spell that Angelina would cast on herself.

As Merilee finished her snack, Angelina set up a magical circle of protection. Merilee didn't bother trying to memorize what her sister had done, as she might have when she'd been human. She couldn't recreate it now.

The circle was at least three feet across, going from one counter to the island, completely covering the floor. The symbols that decorated the edges of it all looked squiggly to Merilee, like ancient Chinese symbols. Angelina had sprinkled a red powder across the floor and the symbols had automatically formed out of it.

Merilee had assumed that the red powder was some sort of colored chalk. But her nose told her differently, that blood was mixed in there as well. Not human, but maybe goat blood.

Angelina had certainly upped her magical game at some point. When had she started using blood, though?

When Angelina was finished, she looked at Merilee, then pointed imperiously to the center of the circle.

Appeared that Merilee was getting the spell cast on her. While Angelina had said that she believed that it was Merilee, she wasn't taking any chances. Hence, the powerful protection circle, not so much to keep Merilee safe, but to protect Angelina in case Merilee wasn't what she appeared to be.

Fine. At least Merilee would be able to talk to her sister for a brief time.

Her fur stood on end as she passed across the edge of it. Interesting. The energy of the protection spells that Angelina had used pulsed hard around her, making a roaring noise like an ocean wave. The spells had a distinctly human scent to them, like burnt plastic and hot metal. The smell stung and made her eyes water unpleasantly.

She felt the circle enclose around her tightly, like a trap that had just been set.

But surely Angelina wasn't setting a trap, right? She was just trying to protect herself from the unknown.

To distract herself, Merilee thought about what she would do for a protective circle. What kinds of spells would she use as a cat? Something more natural, that was for certain. It would carry the scent of lavender and pine she suddenly knew. It wouldn't be this big, three feet across. No, it would only be big enough for her to lie down in, or to protect a litter of kittens.

Did she want kittens? Having kids had never been an option, not really, when she'd been a human. She'd had no interest in raising a family. Now, though…

Thoughts to explore another time.

Merilee sat in the center of the protective circle, placing her butt on the cold, hard tile floor, her tail automatically wrapping around her front paws. She looked up at Angelina, who appeared to be waiting for a sign.

"Mrrrow," Merilee said as firmly as she could.

She was ready.

Angelina nodded in return, and started the vocalization spell.

Merilee braced herself for the onslaught of magic that descended upon her.

CHAPTER 12

Merilee resisted the urge to start grooming herself as the spell finished. It felt as though she'd just walked through a series of sticky cobwebs. Though she hadn't ever thought about it, as a cat, she naturally felt lighter on her feet.

The spell had tied her more tightly to the ground.

She shook herself and tried to speak. "Mrrow?" was what she heard. But superimposed on her usual inquiry she heard the words, "Understand me?"

"Yes! Yes, I do," Angelina said, sounding relieved.

Huh. Had she been worried that the spell wouldn't have worked? She was the Great Angelina! Master Witch! Everything she ever turned her hand to transmuted into gold. Didn't it?

"What happened to you? Why are you a cat? Why haven't you changed back? Are you cursed?" Angelina asked, the words tripping over themselves.

Merilee shook her head. The answers to those questions weren't as important as warning her sister. "No matter," she said. "You are in danger!"

"What do you mean?" Angelina said sharply.

"Three men. Try to kidnap me. I transform. Escape," Merilee said. She couldn't express herself fully, even with this spell. Besides, they were just words. As a cat, she was already used to speaking with her whole body. How she held her shoulders, the tilt of her head, the angle of her tail, all added nuance and shaded the meaning of what she said.

Things she was certain that Angelina was ignoring. And quite possibly, would never bother learn to hear.

"By turning yourself into a cat?" Angelina guessed.

"Yes," Merilee said. She couldn't help but purr. She really had transformed into a magnificent creature.

"But why not change back?" Angelina asked. That seemed to be a sticking point with her.

Merilee gave a loud kitty sigh. "I died. The bad men killed me. I lost one life. One of nine."

"They killed you?" Angelina said, outraged.

Finally, Merilee was getting the type of reaction from Angelina that she'd been wanting.

"Yes," Merilee said. "Cats have nine lives. Eight now. Humans only have one."

The shocked look on Angelina's face said it all. Dismay and sorrow weren't far behind.

"I'll find a way to bring you back," Angelina said. "I swear, I'll—"

"No," Merilee said firmly. "What about you? Why bad men want to hurt you?"

"I don't know," Angelina said.

Merilee could tell she was lying. Angelina might have been able to fool Merilee when she'd been human. But as a cat, she could see it easily. It was in all that body language that most humans didn't know how to hide. As a cat. She could now effortlessly read it.

"Tell me," she insisted. "Why did Thing Two warn you? What they want you to do?"

Angelina sighed. "It's a long story," she said after a few minutes.

Merilee sat down fully on the floor, her front paws tucked under her. "I have time."

"The spell will dissipate soon," Angelina said.

"I understand you," Merilee said. "You just too dumb to understand me."

Angelina rolled her eyes. "Right. Because I'm the one who's transformed herself into a cat and now can't change back."

"Don't want to change back," Merilee said stubbornly. The *mrrow* she gave sounded quite emphatic to her ears.

"Why not?" Angelina said.

Merilee looked up at her sister. "Stronger magic this way," she said.

"What, you have stronger magic now?" Angelina said, completely bewildered. It obviously wasn't the answer she was expecting at all.

"Yes," Merilee said. She stood up again, then turned, and walked right out of the protective circle, away from Angelina.

Magic crackled through her fur, shocking her. Fire burned the pads of her feet. All she could smell was melting wax and burning hair.

But it only lasted a few moments. Then the unpleasantness was over and she was through.

"No!" Angelina shouted. She sounded panicked.

"Mrrow?" Merilee said. She heard no human words over her cat expression. Was the vocalization spell limited to the circle? That seemed strange.

She tried to speak again, but the sound caught in her throat. As did her breath.

She swallowed hard against an unknown lump that blocked her airway.

"NOOOOO!" wailed Angelina. She couldn't just walk through the protective circle. It filled the kitchen floor. She raced around the island, coming up the other way.

Merilee tried again to breathe. She crouched down, closer to the cold tile, her head suddenly dizzy. Her lungs were on fire.

This was far too familiar a feeling. It reminded her of the horrible (horrible!) drowning that the thugs had forced on her.

She glared at Angelina, who was frantically trying to cast another spell. Hopefully a healing one.

Dark spots appeared in front of Merilee's eyes. She grew dizzy.

She still couldn't breathe.

What had Angelina done to her?

Tears streamed down Angelina's face. She raced through the words of the spell, but Merilee knew that she'd finish too late.

Far too late.

Merilee felt her knees grow weak and she collapsed onto her side, on the kitchen floor.

All she wanted was a little air. Just a little. A hint to help her keep going.

Nothing came but blackness.

~

This time, the blue oval that appeared before Merilee floated just above Angelina's kitchen floor. The protection spell still glowed an ominous red to the side.

Angelina was nowhere to be seen.

Merilee knew that she was about to lose another life. It

was the only way she could get back to the world, by stepping through the portal.

Damn it! Why would Angelina kill her that way? Was she so afraid? What had Merilee ever done to her?

She was almost tempted to not step through the oval. Almost. It would serve Angelina right, to have to live forever with the fact that she'd killed her baby sister.

But by staying dead, Merilee felt certain that she was killing her sister as well.

They needed each other in order to get them both out of the mess that Angelina was in.

Merilee knew that this time, going through the oval and returning to life wasn't going to be as straight-forward. It might look as though all she had to do was to step through that portal.

Nothing this difficult was going to be easy, or without consequences.

However, Merilee had to save Angelina. If nothing else, she'd have the upper hand for the rest of her life (actually, all seven lives) to tease her sister about killing her.

Merilee gave one last, loud kitty sigh, then stepped through the portal.

This time, it wasn't just passing through ice. It was walking on sharp icicles, each step cutting into the soft pads of her feet. The same feeling of her fur being torn out occurred. She suspected that if she kept doing this, her luxurious coat would turn thin and ratty. Despite the cold that froze her bones, her lungs were still on fire as she struggled to breathe. The smell of rotting meat accompanied her, clinging to her whiskers.

It took less time to get through the portal, or at least that was how Merilee felt. After a few steps, she saw her choice.

To the left lay that warm, inviting light. If she stepped

that way, put even a single paw into it, she'd be whisked away to someplace blissful and restful.

Instead, she turned and went the other way, toward the bluish haze that danced just on the horizon. As she walked, she felt as though she passed through a watery curtain, the cool liquid condensing on her fur.

"Mrrow?" she murmured sleepily as she felt her soul return to her prone body. She no longer lay on the kitchen floor, but on Angelina's lap.

Her fur was wet with Angelina's tears.

"Oh, baby," Angelina muttered. "I'm sorry. I'm so very, very sorry."

Merilee tried to open her eyes, but that would take too much effort. She was here now. She was warm and safe.

When the morning came, it would be time enough to yell at her sister. For now, she could sleep.

LIFE THREE

CHAPTER 13

Merilee woke curled up on a strange towel. It was soft but stank of fabric softener. Yuck. She sneezed once before she fully opened her eyes.

She appeared to be in some sort of cardboard box. The bottom of the box had been covered in towels.

What, she didn't rate a pillow? She was going to have some *words* with Angelina about that.

She gave a heart-felt kitty sigh and stretched out one paw, then the next, feeling her way back into her body. She still felt, well, unsettled, after her latest death experience.

What the hell had Angelina been thinking, putting a death trap on her protective circle? Was that any way to treat her sister? What kind of dark magic had Angelina gotten mixed up with?

Merilee stood and stretched a little more, before standing on her rear paws and peering out over the top of the box.

Good. She was in the living room, on the coffee table in the center of the room. At least Angelina hadn't tried closing her in a closet or a bedroom. She sniffed.

Angelina was nearby. Merilee could smell her sister's tears.

There she was. Curled up on her couch, sound asleep.

She'd cast a lot of strong magic that afternoon. Even the Mighty Angelina would be tired after that.

Merilee easily jumped out of the box, though when she landed on the coffee table she felt a twinge of something in her left hip. It wasn't much. Just a slight warning that her cat body had changed. Aged, for want of a better term, with her second death.

She really wasn't looking forward to what would happen when she lost her next life. Going through that portal, coming back to life, was just going to get harder and harder.

After one more really good stretch, which still felt so much better in a cat's body than in a human's, Merilee leaped from the coffee table onto the couch. She daintily walked over Angelina's legs, up to her chest, butting up against her chin.

"Yes, I'm awake," Angelina said. She sounded more tired and resigned than resentful.

Slowly, one hand came up and started petting Merilee. She arched into the touch, shifting around, trying to get Angelina to pet the right spots.

Ah. There. Angelina had finally figured out how to skritch her under her chin.

Purrrrrrrrrrrrrrr.

When Merilee was done, she shook her head, a clear indication that Angelina should stop petting her now.

Of course, Angelina paid no heed to Merilee's desires.

Merilee leaned away, trying to get away from the annoying fingers. Finally, she put a paw up to stop Angelina.

"Enough, huh?" Angelina said. She sighed and dropped her hand.

Merilee lay down on Angelina's chest, her paws folded up underneath her. "Mrrow?" she inquired.

Another deep sigh from Angelina, that Merilee felt, making her rise and lower slightly.

"I suppose you want to hear why those, what, things? thugs? have been coming after me," Angelina said.

"Mrrow!" Merilee said, hoping that the sound contained the right emphasis. She wasn't planning on moving until Angelina complied.

"Fine," Angelina said. "Magic should never be used for material, personal gain," she said slowly.

Merilee nodded. She knew that. All the witches who considered themselves "good" witches lived life that way, all of her cousins. Witches could sometimes use their power to help friends (and only now did Merilee think guiltily of her friends—what were they thinking? She was supposed to go out for drinks on Friday, but she had no idea what day it was currently).

Normally, a witch's power was used to ease her life along, and to help her family. Not to make herself rich.

Not if she was a good witch.

"Mrrow?" Merilee asked. *And?*

"And I may have strayed slightly from the path," Angelina said. "It wasn't much, at first."

Merilee didn't say anything, but she knew that she was radiating disapproval.

"I started working with Richard Keebler," Angelina said. "Do you know him? Have you heard of him?"

Merilee started to shake her head, but then paused. The name did sound vaguely familiar.

"He's made huge donations to local charities," Angelina hurried on. "The Mayo Center, downtown. And the symphony. And the new children's hospital. He's done some marvelous work for the city."

Merilee tilted her head to the side, waiting for the other shoe to drop.

"He makes his money on the stock market," Angelina said. "And he's a witch. A Seer, actually. A powerful one."

Merilee gave Angelina a disapproving "Mrrrow." Just because he gave his money away didn't necessarily mean he was a good witch. Plus, if he were that good of a Seer, why did he need Angelina?

"He can't actually use his talents on the stock market," Angelina hurried to clarify. "He primarily is aware of natural events, such as when the next earthquake is going to happen in Taiwan, or the next volcanic eruption in Iceland."

Merilee nodded, needing for Angelina to go on.

"I'm not a Seer either," Angelina said slowly. "But I'm really good at forecasting spells."

"Mrrow?" Merilee asked, confused. Weren't they the same thing?

"No," Angelina said. "A Seer sees things without additional spells. A witch who does forecasting must cast the spell. Spells. And the ingredients are expensive." She sighed. "Richard gave me the money to try. And I was so successful at first! I made him good money. Really good money. I didn't keep any of it. I channeled it all to his accounts, so that he could continue to give it to charities."

Merilee shook her head. Sounded like the start of a slippery slope.

"But something I didn't know about the forecasting spells —they take more and more power to perform. The first few are easy. They grow progressively more difficult to cast. They take longer, and use more ingredients as well."

Angelina looked away from Merilee. She seemed… ashamed? Really? The Great Angelina?

"When Richard suggested that I use an alternative spell, I glomped onto it. Hard. I was so caught up in the excitement of what I was doing. It was such an adrenaline rush to see the money pouring in. I was winning, in a big way, you know?"

"Mrrow," Merilee said, trying to at least sound sympathetic. She wasn't as driven as her sister. Never had been. Didn't quite get it, to be honest. Even when she'd been human.

"But it was dark magic," Angelina confessed. Tears glittered in her eyes. She brushed them away with the back of her hand. "And I…at first I didn't care."

Merilee pushed herself forward, butting her head against Angelina's hand.

Angelina gave Merilee a watery smile and awkwardly pet Merilee's head.

"I know. I know. I was being stupid," Angelina said.

"Mrrow," Merilee said, though she could tell Angelina couldn't necessarily read the nuance that Merilee had put into the vocalization.

Her sister had been more stubborn than stupid, probably. As she said, she'd been winning. That had really been all that mattered to her.

"Then, I don't know. It was something Sue said, about one of the companies that I was shorting, something about a meme-stock, that made me start to track the money." Angelina's expression changed, her face taking on that more familiar anger. "Richard had really snowed me. He was pulling in a lot, *a lot* more money than I thought. Like, twenty times more. I wasn't just making money for charities. I was lining his pockets, but good."

Merilee nodded. Though she'd never met this Richard, she wasn't surprised. Nothing good came out of trying to work around the system. Particularly not for good witches.

"So I quit. Or I tried to quit. Richard wouldn't just let me walk away, though. I was too good, too valuable of an asset," Angelina said bitterly.

Merilee could very well imagine just how well Angelina had taken to being told that she was an *asset*. No, the Great Angelina always ran the show, whether she was in the spotlight or not. She wasn't merely a side player.

"Richard offered me money. Told me that he'd put aside more money for charity. All the right things. I didn't trust him, though. Not after he'd broken his word that way."

Angelina gave another deep sigh, lifting Merilee up and down again. "Richard eventually appeared to give up. I thought he'd figured out that I'd crossed too many lines and I was fighting to make my way back. I wasn't going to continue down that path. But it appears that he hadn't."

Merilee nodded. No, Richard had instead hired three thugs to "get" her. Probably kidnap her, and hold her as leverage against Angelina.

"I didn't think they'd come after you," Angelina said, reaching up to softly run her fingers along Merilee's jowl line.

It felt so good, Merilee immediately started to rumble.

Angelina smiled. "You know, I've always considered myself a dog person, not a cat person."

Merilee just glared at her sister. *You don't say.* It was probably one of the reasons why the pair of them had never gotten along.

Angelina like dogs, while Merilee, at some level, had always been a cat.

"But I can understand the appeal, at least when you purr like that," she continued with a small smile.

Merilee closed her eyes and pushed her head further into Angelina's hand. That felt so good. Like the best massage she'd ever had, and it was merely her inexperienced sister running her fingers across her fur.

Just imagine what someone who liked cats, who was good with them, who could understand them, would be like!

After a few more extended moments of sheer bliss, Merilee shook herself, dislodging Angelina's hands.

"Mrrow?" she asked, hoping that Angelina could follow her. What about their mother? Or cousins? Or other people Angelina might be close to, who lived nearby?

"What, are you hungry? Thirsty? Do you need to use the toilet, or something? God, I'm just not set up to take care of an animal!"

Merilee growled at that. She wasn't an animal, or at least not *merely* a cat. She still had her entire human persona. Mostly. Some bits might have been rubbed off during the transition, but other, better bits had been included instead.

After shaking her head a few times, Angelina finally shrugged. "I don't understand," she said.

Merilee stared into Angelina's eyes, trying to force that one word out so that Angelina would hear it.

Mom.

"Oh. Oh!" Angelina said, finally understanding. "They're fine. Richard can't get them, can't use them as leverage. While you were recovering last night, I told Mom to take a long vacation at the cabin. And to invite the cousins along. No one can get near them. No, it's just us, for now."

"Mrrow," Merilee said. As it should be. They were more than enough of a match for some bad guys.

She stood and stretched on Angelina's chest, arching and stretching, before delicately leaping down.

Yes, she probably should go outside for a bit. While she was certain she could use a human toilet, it wouldn't be easy or comfortable.

She walked over to the front door, looked at it, then back at Angelina.

"Fine, I get the hint," Angelina said. She heaved herself

up from the couch. "What time is it? Goodness, it's after midnight!" She shook her head. "I'm going to be a mess at work tomorrow."

Merilee wanted to fuss at Angelina. She needed to take a few days off so that she could work on the problems she was currently facing.

However, something had caught Merilee's attention.

Something bad was outside.

Something waiting for them.

Merilee started to hiss.

CHAPTER 14

"What is it?" Angelina said. "What's the matter?"

Merilee felt all the hair rise up along her spine. Her tail puffed out, growing twice as big. She made a low growling noise, deep in her chest. Her claws extended and extracted.

She wasn't sure what menace lay outside the door, but she had no doubt that something was there. Something bigger than just the three thugs.

"Just a moment," Angelina said. She walked away, into the bathroom, then came back, carrying a hand mirror. It looked quite plain, with a golden handle. The mirror itself was barely the size of Angelina's outstretched hand.

"Do you remember the *ba gua* I have above the doorframe?" Angelina asked.

Merilee shook her head.

"I knew that it really wasn't going to keep anything like monsters or demons, or even evil spirits from entering my house," Angelina explained. "They actually don't care if they see themselves in a mirror."

Interesting. Where had Angelina gained that knowledge?

While there were some witches dedicated to fighting the creatures of the night, that had never been the case with their family. They were more healers and seers, with a long history of witchcraft, going back to the seventeenth century.

"But I can use the mirror in the center of the *ba gua* for seeing things outside," Angelina continued.

She held the mirror flat, then murmured something quietly while waving her other hand over the surface of the mirror.

"Mrrow?" Merilee said. She stood up on her rear paws and balanced her front paws on Angelina's leg, trying to get a better look.

"Right," Angelina said after a moment. She tried to squat, then finally sat down on the couch.

Merilee stepped on her sister's thigh, then into her lap.

Angelina blew out her breath. "I'm just going to have to get used to this, aren't I?" she groused.

Merilee wasn't sure exactly what she meant. Having a gorgeous, sleek, remarkable cat in her lap wasn't something that anyone should have to *work* at getting used to.

But before she could berate her sister for her lack of understanding, Merilee caught sight of the mirror.

Fog rolled across the surface of the glass, maybe two inches high. Was it supposed to do that?

Merilee looked up at Angelina and saw that she was moving her lips in a spell. So yeah, it appeared that way.

She looked back down at the mirror, watching with fascination as the fog cleared and suddenly she had a bird's eye view of the front yard.

There, to the side, stood the boss.

Merilee found herself growling again. She tapped that side of the mirror, hoping that Angelina could see the man standing there as well.

"I see him," Angelina said.

The smell of ozone rose quickly as Angelina grew angrier. "But what's he doing?" she said after a moment.

"Mrrow," Merilee said firmly.

"Spell?" Angelina asked. At Merilee's nod, Angelina continued. "Is he magical?"

Merilee shook her head. No, none of the thugs had struck her as magical, not in the least.

Then how was he casting a spell? That made no sense.

"It isn't a spell he's casting," Angelina said after a few more moments of peering at the mirror. "He's placing an amulet."

"Mrrow?" Merilee asked.

"I don't know what kind. I'm assuming nothing good," Angelina said.

The man drew runes in a circle underneath one of the nearby pine trees. Would they hold any power? Or was Richard counting on just the presence of them attracting something?

Merilee watched, curious, as the man placed the amulet in the center of the circle he'd drawn. He waved his hands a couple of times over the spot, as if he were actually doing an incantation.

But he had no power. Though Merilee couldn't smell him, she was certain of it.

She knew of no spell that would allow one person to channel another's magic. Say, a powerful witch and his or her minion.

But maybe that was exactly what was happening. Maybe someone with dark magic could do such a thing.

Merilee was about to ask Angelina about it, when the man abruptly bent over, scooped up the amulet, and threw it hard, up into the branches of the tree.

"What did he do that for?" Angelina asked.

Merilee kept her snort to herself. She had a very good

idea why, though of course her sister wouldn't see why immediately.

After all, Angelina always had thought of herself as the most important one.

However, Richard and his thugs had other plans.

The amulet was probably powerful. Enough so that it would be dangerous to leave it there in that tree.

Angelina couldn't climb up to get it. And witches couldn't fly.

However, Merilee could easily face down that tree. She was going to have to go fetch that amulet.

No matter what the cost.

CHAPTER 15

"No," Angelina said. "Absolutely not. I am not risking you, or perhaps you losing another life."

Merilee sat there patiently, waiting next to the door.

The boss of the thugs had already made his smirking way out of the front garden. As far as Merilee could smell, or Angelina could see, none of the thugs remained.

"You don't have to do this," Angelina said. "It's obviously a trap. For you. That other thug, Thing Two I think you called him? Saw you the other day. Must think that I have a familiar as well. Of course they'd be out to get you!"

Merilee didn't say anything. She merely turned her head, looked toward the door, then back up at Angelina again.

Her sister couldn't keep her trapped inside the house forever. Merilee would make her life a living hell if she tried. Her claws were more than a match for Angelina's fancy leather furniture. Though she wasn't really considering it, if push came to shove, she would use Angelina's bed for her litterbox.

And she was certain that there were a whole bunch of

other things that her cat nature would suggest to her, once she really got going along the path of revenge.

Like perhaps throwing up in Angelina's fancy leather boots…

"Just—just let me do a protection spell on you first, okay?" Angelina said.

"Mrrooowww!" Merilee said, as forcefully negative as she could get, shaking her head hard.

Angelina hadn't meant to kill her that first time. Merilee knew that. Angelina had just been protecting herself.

However, her sister had also turned toward darker magic. Merilee had always heard that it would creep into the rest of Angelina's magic as well. There was no such thing as "just a few" dark magic spells.

Until Angelina properly cleansed herself (and no, not even a tongue bath from a cat would do it) she needed to avoid using magic.

Particularly when it came to casting spells on her younger sister.

"Fine," Angelina huffed. "You go and lose another life. I suppose you can afford it."

She opened the door angrily.

Merilee gave her sister a good dose of stink-eye before she walked across the threshold and out the door, holding every inch of herself with great dignity.

Angelina didn't understand what it had cost Merilee to die and come back. Maybe some time Merilee could explain it to her, tell her how much it had hurt, and how each death was going to plague her, age her, until she was an ancient, decrepit old cat.

The smells of the night assailed Merilee before she reached the bottom step. There was the constant stink of humans, of course, as well as their vehicles. But layered through that were sweeter scents, like the green smell of the dew-speckled lawn, the teasing aroma of a nearby mouse, the more acidic odor of the anthill on the side of the driveway.

Plus, there was a soft breeze that ruffled through her fur, giving her a delightful sensation. The night wasn't too dark, or at least she didn't think so, once her night vision really kicked in. Though the air was cool—she could feel it against her wet nose—she wasn't cold in the least. Mind you, if she was going to stay out all night she would be tempted to change back into her white-furred white-haired version.

Maybe she should do that anyway, after she had the amulet. It might give Angelina a good fright.

Merilee bobbed her head up and down as she giggled, wending her way over to the tall pine tree.

As a human, she hadn't ever paid that much attention to the tree. Sure, she knew the lore about pines. They were one of the guardian trees. It took some work to bend a pine tree to do your will. If you messed up the spell, the tree was likely to turn against you. She'd heard more than one fairy tale about the evil that pine trees could do.

These days, most witches didn't bother trying to enchant the trees around them. Instead, they relied on modern, mundane technology, things like locks and alarms.

Kids these days.

Merilee found herself snickering again.

She reached the base of the tree and looked up. Now, where was that amulet?

It took her a few moments before she spotted it. The amulet didn't shine with magic, no. Instead, it sucked in the light all around it. It glowered darkly, like a cold shadow, caught and held in the high branches.

Then, Merilee looked around for the set of runes that the boss had drawn into the ground. They also weren't easy to see at first. Again, she finally found them not due to the magic they exuded, but the way that they sucked up any stray light or magic that happened to be floating around.

She reached out a cautious paw to swipe at the first symbol. A shiver went all the way up her arm, making her back arch.

Yuck.

However, once she touched it, she realized that there were other spots in the yard, where similar circles and runes had been drawn.

Just one little circle wouldn't do anything to Angelina and her power. But a whole series of them? They were surely draining her sister, one little cut at a time.

And the presence of them might call something big and nasty to the yard.

Merilee didn't have the time, patience, or energy to destroy every single one of those. Angelina would have to do that work.

Later, though.

Merilee returned her attention to the tree. She paused, looking up, planning her line of attack. She wriggled her butt before she sprang upwards, her paws effortlessly hooking into the rough bark of the pine.

Ewww. It was sticky.

She was either going to have to spend a lot of time grooming herself later, or maybe she'd have to wipe all the excess gunk off her paws onto Angelina's nice leather furniture.

Or maybe both.

Angelina had killed her once already, after all. And Merilee still owed her for that.

It didn't take much time or effort at all for Merilee to reach the branch where the amulet hung. However, it was much further out from the trunk than she'd originally believed.

She was going to have to balance and walk carefully along the tree branch to get out to it.

As a human, she might have already given up. There was no way to reach that amulet, all the way out there. Even if she'd brought up something like a broom, she still couldn't have knocked it down.

As a cat, Merilee considered her position, calculating where she was and where she wanted to go.

She *really* didn't want to just walk along that branch. Something was warning her against such a course.

No, the longer she was up here, in the tree, the more at risk she was. The breeze that had originally been delightful was now cold. She found herself growling softly, almost under her breath. Her claws dug in more tightly to the bark, as if she were suddenly afraid that she could get knocked off.

Merilee shook her head, considered her relative position again, before she turned and flung herself into the darkness, headlong against the oily shadows that had begun gathering around the amulet.

CHAPTER 16

It wasn't Merilee's imagination that the branch dipped dangerously when she landed.

Whatever magic that amulet contained was slowly leaching out the life of everything around it.

Damn it! Was it powerful enough to twist the spirit of the pine that lived inside the tree? Or had the tree already been corrupted, with all the dark circles of negative power that had been placed around Angelina's yard?

Merilee wasn't certain. All she knew was that she had little time to grab that amulet and haul it out of the tree.

Fortunately, her first jump had landed her only a couple of feet away from where the dark leather thong holding the amulet had been snagged.

Merilee took one step forward from her crouched position, then another.

She felt the shaking of the tree before she felt the powerful wind that sprang up out of nowhere.

While the amulet itself probably wasn't that strong, chances were that some heavy-duty spells surrounded it.

Merilee clung to the branch as it was tossed up and down.

The amulet also bounced along. But Merilee's luck wasn't good enough for her to be able to shake it loose.

Now that she was closer, she could see the amulet itself. It had been forged out of a golden metal, though she doubted that it was made from solid gold. If she was remembering correctly, metallurgy combined with magic was always a melding of ingredients. Very few, if any, witches would bother enchanting something that was made out of a single ingredient. It wasn't worth the cost of ingredients or power. Using different substances was made an enchanted item more effective, and a good witch could hang separate spells off of each material, weaving them together into a powerful artifact.

She could see the raised runes circling the edge of the amulet. They resembled the runes that she'd seen Angelina use for her protection circle.

Probably not a good thing.

The amulet had a simple hole drilled through the top of it, and it hung by what looked like a leather thong. She sniffed, teasing apart the magical smells that came to her—silvery metal, blunted cork, and even human sweat—but no blood.

This amulet sucked away at the light and at magic. It wasn't some kind of container for an even greater monster.

Merilee wasn't sure why she knew that so certainly, but she trusted her cat senses.

Nothing about this amulet was alive. She'd bet at least one life on that.

Slowly, Merilee inched along the branch. She was grateful for all six of her claws, giving her solid purchase against the wood.

Just a few more inches…

She caught the scent of the fire before she saw it. It was smoldering beneath the tree.

Was that what those dark spots were supposed to do? Could they be used not merely to suck away Angelina's magic, but to act like portals, so this Richard guy—Rick, no, *Dick*, Dick the Elf—could send fire through them?

It took her two breaths to realize that the smoke smelled wrong.

There was no fire. It was an illusion.

One that would probably fool Angelina into stepping outside. Maybe be stripped of all her power.

Merilee had to hurry.

"Merilee!" Angelina called from the door of her house.

Merilee yowled as loudly as she could.

Stay there.

Of course, her stupid sister didn't hear her. Or maybe she did, and just ignored Merilee's warning.

"You need to get down out of that tree right now!"

Merilee rolled her eyes, though Angelina couldn't see her. She knew that.

She reached out one paw to tap at the leather of the thong holding the amulet, not touching it with her actual toe bean, just with a claw.

The shock that ran through her was more shivery than Merilee was comfortable with.

But she had to get that amulet out of the tree, so that Angelina would go back inside. Stop endangering herself needlessly.

Trust that Merilee could do this.

"Hurry!" Angelina said.

Merilee took a moment to peer down. Angelina stood at the base of the tree, gazing up. Even from this distance, Merilee could tell that Angelina's eyes were slightly glazed.

The fake fire and smoke had dissipated. Probably something that Angelina had taken care of.

However, the magic holes scattered across the yard were doing their work. What was Angelina seeing, as her head suddenly started swiveling left and right?

Merilee tried to hook the leather with a claw. No go. Now, the amulet was twisting away from her, carried on its own wind.

Damn it! Merilee knew what she was going to have to do. She didn't like it, not one bit.

But there was nothing else she could think of. Not if she was going to save her sister.

Merilee pushed herself forward abruptly. Now, she was directly over the amulet, still swinging madly in a breeze that Merilee didn't feel.

Slowly, Merilee leaned over the edge. She felt herself going even as she tried to balance.

However, just before she fell, she managed to get the leather thong in her mouth.

It was *nasty*. Like a dead mouse that had been killed on the edge of the highway, then left to rot in the sunshine for a week. The leather itself crawled over her tongue, as if it were made up of a living worm, trying to wiggle its way down her throat. The weight of the amulet dragged her down, toward the ground. Even if she hadn't been falling, the amulet would have tipped her over.

For a few moments, it felt to Merilee as though she were flying. She twisted herself naturally, turning her face toward the ground, using her tail to orient her body so all four paws were stretched out.

Was she actually going to make it?

A moment before impact, something grabbed her out of the air.

Ooofff.

Angelina held Merilee in her arms, drawing her in, close to her chest.

"You did it!" Angelina exclaimed happily.

Merilee twisted immediately. She needed to get down, now.

"All right, you ungrateful wretch," Angelina grumbled.

Merilee raced back toward the house, bounding up the steps toward the open door.

She paused on the threshold, looking back hopefully at her sister.

Nope. Angelina was still standing there, next to that tree. She appeared to be plucking things out of the air.

Was she catching other versions of Merilee?

With a sigh, Merilee spat out the leather thong. Yuck. She licked her fur a few times, trying to get the taste out of her mouth. That thing was just gross.

Fortunately, it just lay there, like an actual inanimate thing. Had the magical protections that Angelina put around her house neutralized the thing? Merilee could only hope so.

She paused for a moment, taking another deep breath, before bounding down the stairs.

Time to save her sister. Again.

CHAPTER 17

This time, as Merilee made her way across the lawn, she felt as though she were stepping through sheets of fog. Gauzy cold curtains stood between her and her sister.

And Angelina was definitely trapped inside them.

They were drawing closer to her sister, as well as to herself. Would they end up wrapping around her tightly, holding her in a cocoon, until some bigger, more evil bastard could get to her?

Not if Merilee could help it.

Angelina had at least finally woken to the fact that she might be in trouble. She tried using her puny human nails to shred the attacking veils.

Merilee sprang into action, yowling. She racked her claws through the first line of fog, then the next.

They were shivery cold, freezing her paw. The ice sunk deep into her bones. She knew that eventually, the cold would overwhelm her.

Good thing that she had thick fur.

It took her only a moment to transform into the white cat that she'd originally been. That helped tremendously. She moved like a white wraith across the yard, destroying every veil that she could reach.

Angelina was also attacking the veils.

Now, if Merilee could only get her sister to move *away* from the tree, out of the yard…The protections of Angelina's house would help drive back whatever was attacking them.

Merilee yowled, yelling at Angelina, saying as clearly as she could that her sister needed to run.

Of course, Angelina didn't understand her. Or if she did, she chose to ignore the warning that Merilee was *obviously* giving.

No, the Great Angelina had to save the day, and do all the work herself.

At least she stopped trying to use her hands to destroy the veils. Instead, she called up some lightning, sending out blinding streams of it, tearing through the cold and ghostly sheets.

It wouldn't be enough. No, Angelina either needed to destroy all the hidden pockets of darkness, or else leave the damned yard.

Merilee finally fought her way to Angelina's side, butting her head against her sister's leg, trying to get her attention, to get her *away* from the circle of runes that were beside her.

"I'll protect you," Angelina growled.

Merilee rolled her eyes. That was *not* what she wanted, not in the least.

She wrapped on paw around Angelina's ankle, then *pulled* with all her might, without extending her claws. Much. Okay, just enough of a hint to get a good hold of Angelina's sock.

Angelina looked down. "Oh. Oh!" she said seeing the circle.

With a blast of strong wind, Angelina smeared one of the runes, breaking the magical circle.

The area underneath the pine tree grew brighter.

"Mrrow!" Merilee said loudly. She looked at the house, then back at Angelina.

"I can't leave these things here," Angelina said through gritted teeth as she flung out another white streak of lightning.

Merilee didn't know how to convince her sister that yes, she could. She didn't actually need to be in the thick of things. She could stand next to her house, be protected by those spells, and from there, send out her winds.

Why didn't she see that?

Right. Because the gauze was hiding her sight.

Merilee went over to the closest circle of darkness and tapped at one of the runes with a paw.

Ouch. That one was stronger. Had it been there longer? Or had someone with more magical strength drawn it?

Merilee didn't smell anyone other than the three thugs in the yard. Maybe one of them was a better minion, could channel the dark magic better.

A bolt of lightning seared the air beside Merilee. She yowled and leaped to the side.

That had been close. Too close.

She peered at Angelina.

Her sister's eyes were more glazed than ever.

She was randomly shooting off streams of strong light. The air sizzled with power, and stank of ozone.

Crap.

Merilee didn't have time to change back into her black-cat self. Instead, she raced for the door of the house, weaving between the dark circles that appeared to be multiplying.

They did suck out the energy that was in the yard, and Angelina was supplying them with more and more power.

However, it was too late, and she knew it. There was no place she could go to avoid Angelina's bolts.

Merilee burned as the lightning blasted her.

Damn it! Her sister had killed her. Again.

Merilee yowled as the darkness took her, her fur on fire.

~

Instead of cold, it was heat that Merilee woke to. She was still outside in the yard. The dark circles were gone. All that remained was that dreadfully familiar portal. Beyond it, the house glowed in the night, like a bright, shining beacon.

What stood on the other side of the portal this time? How hard would it be to go through?

Merilee still stank of burned fur, though her long white coat looked pristine at this time. She realized that her hips worked fine, too. She took a moment luxuriating in a good, proper stretch, both arching and flexing her spine.

Once she went back to the real world, subtle aches that she'd successfully ignored would increase. Maybe even spread to her other joints.

It wouldn't be that bad going through the portal, or at least that was what she tried to convince herself. It was only her third life.

Maybe she could get through this without losing more lives?

Though she was getting the feeling that wouldn't be her fate. No, it was possible that she was supposed to have died that first time, and was now living on borrowed time.

With a sigh, Merilee forced herself forward, her paws dragging as she stepped through the portal.

Brilliant streaks of fire danced across her skin. All her nerves burned and she couldn't help but yowl with disapproval. The pain brought tears to her eyes, hazing her vision. Each step was like walking on hot coals. Her lungs seared. Though she hadn't been aware of breathing before, now she found herself panting, unable to suck in any air. (Had she been breathing? She'd have to check next time.)

It was awful, but she reached the other side quickly enough.

Again, there was the soothing light off to the right. It was closer this time.

The last time, would she have no choice but to step into it?

But Merilee couldn't rest. Not yet. Not while her idiotic older sister was still making a mess of her life.

Merilee turned and walked away from the quiet, healing, blissful light, into the darkness that was her re-entrance to the world.

This time, she'd be more careful. She wouldn't lose another life.

Though she suspected she was lying to herself about that.

LIFE FOUR

Merilee woke up cradled in her sister's lap. It took her a few moments to piece together how she recognized the spot. Maybe it had to do with the soothing hands petting her fur. Or perhaps the salty smell of her sister's tears. It felt good, *right*, to be connected this way to her sibling. No one else's lap would ever feel this way.

"Mrrow?" Merilee said as she came back to consciousness.

Only then did she realize that they were sitting on the top step of the stairs, leading into the house. They weren't inside the house, not yet. The smell of ozone still hung heavily in the air, the summer storm of her sister's familiar anger swirling around them.

"I'm sorry, I'm sorry, I'm so very, very sorry," Angelina said. "I didn't see you. Didn't *recognize* you. You were a black cat before," she added, sounding more accusing now. "Not a white one."

Merilee nodded, her head heavy. All she wanted to do was to go back to sleep, but she knew that she couldn't. She needed to get her sister on the right path, first.

She gave a face-splitting yawn and pushed herself up, out of Angelina's nap. First, she stretched. It still felt amazingly good. However, she could tell that there were now some kinks in her spine, up around her shoulders, signs of age, from losing her third life.

Then, Merilee looked around the yard. Good. All the dark spots were gone. She looked up at Angelina for confirmation.

"Yes, I destroyed them all. From here. I had to get you to safety first. When I blasted you…that broke through whatever spell those assholes had on me. I finally started to see clearly again." She sighed. "I'm sorry," she said again.

"Mrrow?" Merilee said, looking back toward the open door. Why were they out here, and not inside?

"The spells protecting the house are mostly older spells, spells I learned to use before," Angelina said, as if that were an explanation.

"Mrrow?" Merilee wasn't sure what her sister was saying. *Before what?*

"Before Richard," Angelina admitted.

Oh. Oh! Merilee sat back on her hind paws and raised her nose to sniff.

Yup. One, maybe two, of the spells wrapped around the house, protecting it, had a dark scent. She could recognize that now that she knew what she was looking for.

"As long as those are standing, we're both in danger," Angelina said. "I need to break them first, but I need to be outside to do it."

Merilee nodded. She looked expectantly at Angelina.

"All right," Angelina said. She pushed herself up to standing. She swayed slightly.

All the power that Angelina had expended had really drained her. Her face was pale, and dark circles marred the skin under her eyes.

Merilee turned and deliberately faced the yard again. She laid down with her paws folded underneath her, keeping watch while Angelina worked.

It took longer than Merilee expected. Was that because Angelina was so tired? Merilee didn't know what time it was. The smell of the air told her that dawn would be coming soon. She spent a few moments translating that into human —so probably about 3 AM. They'd come out here after midnight, she remembered Angelina saying.

Nothing came at them while Angelina unwove the spells wrapped around her house, then redid them. This time, they were purer, cleaner. They felt right when Merilee rubbed her fur across them.

Angelina was barely able to stay on her feet by the time she finished. Merilee led her inside, pushing the door closed with her tail.

"Mrrow. Mrrow!" Merilee told Angelina.

"Yes, yes, bed now," Angelina said. "I will need to call in sick to work tomorrow."

Merilee just glared at Angelina.

"Fine. I'll send them a text," she said.

Merilee followed Angelina up onto the couch when she sat down with her phone. After Angelina sent the text, Merilee not-so-gently batted at her hand when she swiped open her email app.

"Yes, *Mom*," Angelina groused, closing the program. She looked at Merilee. "Can you sleep…there?" she asked, gesturing vaguely toward the box that Merilee had woken up in earlier.

Merilee stalked across the couch to one of the pillows that was standing on its edge, leaning against the arm of the couch. She daintily pulled it down, then jumped up onto it.

"Towels aren't good enough, huh?" Angelina said. At least she was smiling.

Merilee turned around once, flattening the pillow out a little, before curling up on it. Her tail automatically wrapped around her, coming up to cover her nose. She started purring, both for comfort and to express just how nice this finally felt.

Angelina nodded slowly. "We'll get to the bottom of all this tomorrow. Today. Later," she said with a tired smile.

Merilee took a deep breath and released it before closing her eyes.

Yes, later. They could figure everything out later. After she'd had a good nap.

CHAPTER 19

Merilee woke up with the dawn, of course. She heard all the birds in the trees just outside the windows. Hmmm. All that lovely racket raised the rumbles in her stomach.

She was starving. Likely to fall over in a faint if she didn't get some food into her. Now.

Angelina was still sleeping. Her scent was more relaxed. Merilee hadn't realized that she could tell that before. It was good.

After doing some good stretches, feeling her way back fully into her body, Merilee hopped off the couch and headed into the kitchen.

Was there anything there that she could eat? Anything she could get at without opposable thumbs?

Opening the cabinets above the counter didn't take that much effort. Or even any magic. All she had to do was to stretch up and hook the underside with a claw, then pull.

The cupboards weren't too high up off the countertop. When Merilee stood on her hind paws, she could easily look over the bottom shelf.

There. Above the dishwasher. Tins of tuna.

She may have knocked over a few other things getting to them. It was all right. Angelina appeared to sleep through the noise.

Now, how was she going to open the one she had dropped onto the floor?

There had to be some magical way she could get at the food inside the tin. Really, how hard could this be? She knew how to do it with her human hands. Just raise up the little metal circle.

It took some maneuvering, but eventually, Merilee managed to drag the ring up.

The problem was drawing it back while holding the can stable.

Merilee could grab hold of the ring with her teeth and pull. That wasn't the issue. The whole can would rise up, though. She didn't have the strength to hold onto it while pulling with her teeth, no matter how tightly she held the can, wrapped around the edges of it with her paws.

In frustration, Merilee extended her claws.

It surprised her that they sunk right into the can.

That wasn't normal cat strength. She knew that much. She must be using some level of magic to do that.

Oops. Tuna juice spilled all over the floor when she extracted her claws.

Fortunately, Angelina's floors were immaculately clean, and licking up the tuna juice from them wasn't really a problem, or even that gross.

Merilee experimented, now, puncturing the can, then sliding her paw back, slicing through the metal.

She couldn't just lick where she'd cut the can. The edges were too rough and she'd end up with a bleeding tongue. She kept working at it, eventually opening up the entire side of the tuna so that she could get at it.

After she'd finished her meal, and had given her face and paws a good cleaning, Merilee jumped back up onto the countertop.

There was something else there, in the kitchen, that she needed to find. It had that same nasty smell as the amulet (and what had Angelina done with it? Merilee was going to have to remember to ask later). What secrets did Angelina have hiding in her cupboards?

Merilee opened one, then the next, sniffing her way to the source of the sourness.

There. In the cupboard up above the refrigerator. Where the dust bunnies still reigned. (It made Merilee feel better that even Angelina and her superior cleaning spells managed to miss the top of the fridge.)

This was the cupboard where Angelina kept all her spell ingredients. Merilee hadn't noticed the first time, not when Angelina had been making that protective circle. Then again, she'd been sitting on the floor, next to the sink, not over here, on the far side of the island.

While some of the ingredients here were still good, others smelled as though they'd rotted.

Merilee started sorting through the cupboard, pulling out the items that needed to be thrown away.

If Angelina was going to go back to being a good witch, she needed to get rid of all of these nasty things.

Merilee had no idea what some of these ingredients were. They were kept sealed tight in black glass, and the labels made no sense to her. They weren't in English, or in Spanish, but written in those squiggly characters that Merilee didn't trust.

Despite being sealed, Merilee had no problem figuring out which ingredients needed to go. She pulled them out, one by one, and pushed them over to one side of the fridge.

The good stuff formed a much smaller pile on the other side, or if possible, she left them in the cupboard.

It was only at the end that she accidentally pushed one of the glass jars off the edge of the fridge. It fell with a loud shattering of glass. Noxious fumes rose up from the floor.

Ewwww. It stank like rotten grass on the edge of the river.

The sound woke Angelina up. Merilee felt the energy in the house change.

"Mrrow!" she called to Angelina as her sister walked into the kitchen.

Angelina still wore the over-sized white T-shirt that she'd slept in, along with a pair of light-blue pajama bottoms. She looked like a model, not like someone who'd been comfortably asleep. Even before she'd become a cat, Merilee had always preferred sleeping in as little as possible. She believed in warm, flannel sheets, not clothes for bed.

"What is this?" Angelina said. "Why have you opened up every single cupboard?" She sounded pissed off.

What, had Merilee disrupted some of Angelina's perfect order or something? She actually felt there was something freeing with all the cabinet doors open.

Angelina walked over to the middle of the floor, where the empty tuna can lay accusingly. "If you'd bothered to wake me up, I could have gotten you something to eat," she said, holding up the tuna can, then shaking it at Merilee.

Merilee twitched her tail, the equivalent of a kitty shrug, though she knew that Angelina couldn't read it. Maybe some point, after they'd been living together for a few years, Angelina would be able to understand everything that Merilee said.

And perhaps Dick would just back off without trying to harm the sisters again.

Both proposals had the equivalent chance of success.

"What are you doing up there?" Angelina asked, sounding pissed off.

"Mrrow," Merilee said, waving one of her front paws disapprovingly toward the pile of bad ingredients.

Angelina narrowed her eyes as she looked at the pile. "I see," she said angrily. "And, what, you were just going to knock them off the fridge? One by one, destroy them? You could have hurt yourself, you know. Some of those powders are very toxic. And they're very expensive as well."

Merilee rolled her eyes. No, the first one had been a mistake.

Though if Angelina thought that she could keep them, Merilee might have to deliberately start dropping them.

She reached out a paw and swatted at the nearest one, just to see what Angelina would do.

"No!" Angelina said. She angrily pulled out a stepstool that was tucked next to the refrigerator, then climbed up, obviously intending to scoop up Merilee so she couldn't do any more damage.

Silly human.

Merilee leaped off the side of the fridge, passing over the assortment of "good" jars, landing easily on the countertop.

All right, so she may have squawked a little when she hit. Those hips of hers were just not as good as they'd once been.

Then she jumped down to the floor, and sat at the foot of the stepstool, looking up at Angelina as innocently as you please.

Angelina glared at Merilee, then made as if to step back down.

Merilee swatted at her sister's ankle, preventing her from moving off the ladder. "Mrrow!" she said emphatically.

"What?" Angelina said.

Merilee looked from her sister, up to the pile of "bad" ingredients, then back again.

"I haven't even had my coffee," Angelina complained.

Merilee sneered. What Angelina drank wasn't really coffee. Not as if Merilee had any interest in coffee now. Possibly the cream that she used to put into her own, but not in that soy crap that Angelina used. Or those awful fake flavors.

When Angelina tried to step down again, Merilee swatted at her again. This time, the tips of her claws came out. She didn't slice open Angelina's skin, but she did scratch her slightly.

"Ow!" Angelina said. She glared down at Merilee. "You know I can just jump over you."

Merilee looked at her, then back up at the top of the fridge.

"And I suppose if I do that, you'll jump back up and knock over more things."

Good. Angelina was finally starting to get it. Merilee wasn't kidding. Her sister needed to clean up her act. Right now.

"Fine," Angelina said with a put-upon sigh.

Merilee gave her a six point seven on a scale of ten. Really, Angelina needed to practice her sighs if she wanted to compete with a cat.

"Look, I need to get down and get a bag to put all of these things in," Angelina lied. "Will you at least let me do that?"

Merilee sat back and considered her sister. Again, that whole human lying thing. Angelina was just going to have to learn that Merilee wasn't ever going to be fooled.

Merilee shook her head, and looked off to the side, as if allowing Angelina to descend.

Before her sister put her second foot on the floor, Merilee had already bounded back up, onto the top of the fridge again.

"What?" Angelina said.

Merilee gave a warning growl, and started pushing one of the bottles toward the edge of the fridge.

"All right! All right! You win. I'll go get a bag. Promise."

Merilee merely growled again and maneuvered a second bottle close.

Angelina stalked away, coming back with a plastic garbage bag. At least she was taking throwing these icky things away more seriously.

"Do you know how much money these cost?" Angelina said as she came back up the stepladder.

Merilee continued her growl until Angelina started carefully picking up the bottles and putting them into the bag.

"Wait, even this?" Angelina said, picking up a container that looked as though it contained a hand cream. "This is just a stabilized Vervain. The Enchanter's herb. It's for protection."

Merilee leaned closer to sniff at it delicately. Nope. It was rotten. She shook her head and pushed it toward Angelina.

"Really?" Angelina said. She paused, then opened the jar.

Inside, fungus bloomed across the white cream. Spores puffed up and out, making Angelina cough. Merilee hissed and backed up against the cabinet.

Quickly, Angelina closed the lid on the jar. "It wasn't like that when I made it. I swear to you."

Merilee nodded, then glared at Angelina.

She did realize that the bad ingredients could leach into the good ones, right?

"Fine. I'm getting rid of it all," Angelina said. She hadn't been moving with great speed before, but now, she seemed to be in more of a hurry to dispose of all the items that Merilee had separated out. She didn't stop and question Merilee's opinion again.

"Anything else?" Angelina said after she'd placed all the good ingredients back into the cupboard.

Merilee did another pass through the kitchen, but she didn't find anything. She stalked out of there and started going room-by-room through Angelina's house.

There were only two surprises. One was a pot of something that was definitely *off* in Angelina's bathroom. (Merilee didn't rejoice when she saw that the Perfect Angelina had something of a mess in her makeup cupboard. No, really.)

The other was a second, much smaller amulet. It wasn't inside the house, but instead, stuck to the rear wheel well of Angelina's car.

Someone had placed it there. Was it a tracker? So that Dick could follow Angelina?

Or was it some sort of incendiary device, primed to go off at the most inconvenient time?

Angelina had paled considerably when she pulled the amulet out.

"This isn't good," she said, holding the tiny coin up.

Merilee backed away as winds suddenly lifted Angelina's hair up, as though a fan had just started blowing air into her sister's face.

Angelina's skin started to glow, heating up with her own internal fire as she stared hard at the amulet. A wicked grin crossed her face.

Merilee knew exactly when Angelina crossed the line again, when she went from being a good witch to being one who wasn't as good. She found herself automatically hissing and arching her back, her hackles rising, her tail poofing out.

Angelina paid her no mind, but continued with her spell.

"MRROOOW!" Merilee yelled. She darted forward, slashing at Angelina's ankle.

Angelina laughed, and kicked out at her. "You're just

jealous," she said, her words slurring together as the power grew.

Merilee growled and raced forward again. This time her claws connected solidly with Angelina's skin, drawing blood in five long welts.

"You bitch!" Angelina said. The power she was concentrating between her fingers started to abate, the glow in her face dying out. "I'm going to get you for that!"

Merilee stood her ground as Angelina faced her. Surely her sister wasn't about to kill her again, right?

Fortunately, even the Great Angelina couldn't hold on to two spells at once. Even as she raised her other hand to direct something at Merilee, the spell she was using to destroy the amulet stuttered.

The light faded. Angelina stopped, a puzzled expression on her face. "What was I doing?" she asked, confused.

Merilee knew her sister was back. She walked over next to her, raised up on her hind legs and placed her paws on her sister's knee.

"What is it?" Angelina said. She brought the hand holding the amulet down closer to Merilee's face.

It didn't take much for Merilee to grab the amulet with her teeth and pull it from her sister's hand.

Oh goddess, that tasted *nasty*. Worse than those horrid chemicals she smelled at the back of the garage, the poisons for the mice and such. (Which Angelina was never going to need again, not with Merilee on the job.) Layered over the poison was a sickening burnt taste. Her tongue was instantly coated in greasy ash.

Merilee spit the amulet back out, onto the hard concrete of the garage floor.

"I suppose you can do a better job of destroying that thing?" Angelina asked, the challenge obvious in her tone.

Merilee looked at her, then back at the small amulet. It

was about the size of a dime, and the same color as well. It had a single character carved into the center of it.

She bet it was the character for fire, particularly given the way that Angelina had been reacting to it.

Great. A charm meant to explode and possibly *kill* her sister?

Dick the Elf was going to have to go. And soon.

Merilee circled the amulet once, going what she knew that Angelina would call "clockwise." It had nothing to do with the artificial movements of a mechanical device, and everything to do with undoing the evil manifest in the amulet. She was merely going in the opposite direction to which the thing had been made.

After circling it a second and third time, all the way growling low and deep in her chest, Merilee was ready.

She hesitated for a moment, the reached out with her left paw. Flexing her claws so that they imprisoned the amulet while she wasn't actually touching it, words came to her.

Cold. Light. Ice. Arctic. Chill.

Heat blossomed across all of her paws, but Merilee didn't lift up the one caging the amulet.

Bitter. Raw. Sharp. Glacial. Ice.

She heard, rather than saw, the amulet snap sharply into pieces.

When Merilee lifted her paw, the edges of the amulet were still bleeding red fire, but it oozed out quickly, dissipating to cold, black ash quickly.

Angelina walked over beside her, then knelt down and looked more closely.

"I'm impressed," she said quietly. "I didn't think you

could do that. I, uhm. Could you have done that before? When you'd been a human?"

Merilee shook her head. No, she didn't think so. She had a lot more magic now. It was just different, and she hadn't had time to learn enough about it.

"I see," Angelina said. She blew out her breath. "And you're right. I've been too infected by the dark magic. I can see that now. It didn't even occur to me to freeze the amulet. I'm too drawn up in my own power now to think clearly."

"Mrrrow," Merilee said, butting her head against her sister's knee. Angelina reached out and ran her fingers across Merilee's fur, making Merilee give a soft purr.

Merilee couldn't help it if her sister was an idiot sometimes, if she had crossed that line from stubborn into being stupid.

Fortunately, there was a way back. For both of them.

CHAPTER 20

Merilee followed Angelina back into the house. The spells that encased the house now warmed her in a good way. They were no longer a danger to her or to Angelina.

This was good.

What wasn't good was how Angelina had been losing herself in the dark magic. She was probably further gone than either of them had realized.

Merilee sat to one side of the kitchen, watching Angelina as she cleaned up the broken glass from the bottle Merilee had dropped off the fridge, closed all the cupboard doors, then made herself that concoction that she called coffee (really, it was just a falsely sweetened caffeinated beverage), followed up and made some real food—eggs and bacon, with an English muffin, butter, and sweet strawberry jam that their mother had made the summer before.

"Can I get you anything?" Angelina asked. She held the door of the fridge open so that Merilee could peer inside.

Merilee thought for a moment, then deliberately walked

across the kitchen floor and sat under the sink. She looked at the faucet, then back at Angelina.

"Oh! Water! Of course!" Angelina hurriedly put some in a wide bowl and placed it on the floor.

Merilee delicately slurped up at least half of what she'd been given while Angelina went to sit in the breakfast nook just off the kitchen.

When Merilee was finished, she joined her sister there. She jumped up on one of the chairs, then up onto the table.

Angelina made a disapproving face, but didn't say anything as she continued shoveling food into her mouth. It wasn't until after she was finished and sipping her drink that she finally asked, "So, what are we going to do about Richard and his thugs?"

Merilee caught Angelina's eye, staring hard into them.

Dick the Elf.

Angelina nearly snorted coffee out her nose.

"Right," she said after a few moments recovering. "Dick the Elf. And his henchmen."

Merilee thought for a moment. Then she drew a line with her paw across the table. A short line. Followed by a second that was a bit longer, the third being even longer, and the fourth the longest of all.

"Go after them one at a time, huh? That's smart," Angelina said. She paused, then added, "But we have two other problems on our hands as well. One, I'm far too attracted to the dark magic. I'm not sure how to cleanse myself. Two, you're still a cat. Likely to remain one for a while, at least until I can figure out how to get you some more lives."

Merilee glared at her sister for that last point. She didn't want to go back to being human. Far too much fun being a kitty.

Though maybe it would be nice to have the option, now and again. Honestly, though, she'd be fine if she could be a cat for the rest of her…six lives.

They really were going to have to address cleaning up Angelina's act. How would Merilee go about doing that?

Could she just lick her sister clean? Groom her whole body and drag out the icky stuff with the roughness of her tongue?

It would take a few hours. And Angelina would have to be still for the whole thing. Merilee wasn't even certain that it would work.

As a cat, certainly, that would be how she'd clean herself. And it would possibly do the job.

On a human though…it would just be the first of a few cleansing steps. Angelina would then have to clean herself.

Merilee reached out a paw and touched Angelina's hand when it appeared Angelina was going to speak again.

"What, what is it? You have something, don't you?"

Merilee glared at her sister while she felt her way through the knotty problem.

Out in the backyard, on top of the hill, was the fairy fountain. As a human, Merilee hadn't really believed in fairies. Now, as a cat, she wasn't so sure. There might, indeed, be fairies who lived up there, who might help, after Merilee had worked her tongue all across her sister's skin.

Then there would be a third thing, but Merilee wasn't sure what that would be. Maybe Angelina would be able to figure it out.

It took some time to communicate exactly what Merilee wanted to do, including walking up to the top of the hill in Angelina's backyard.

"That water isn't that clean," Angelina complained about the fountain. "And it's cold."

Merilee just looked at her. *She* wasn't equipped to clean a fountain. As for the cold, well, Angelina might have to deal with that on her own.

"Fine," Angelina said with a sigh.

Merilee barely rated it a five point zero. Seriously, it was like Angelina wasn't even trying.

"I can't just use my magic to clean this, can I?" Angelina asked after a few moments.

Merilee shook her head. Nope.

Not because she was certain that it would be a bad idea, but because it might humble the Mighty Angelina slightly to have to do her own physical labor for a while.

"Fine," Angelina said. She tromped down the hill, back to the house, and reappeared with gloves and a brush. She'd also changed clothes into a sleeveless T-shirt and shorts. It wasn't hot yet, but it was going to get that way by the afternoon.

Merilee kept watch while Angelina cleaned the fountain, scrubbing out the mold that had grown along the edges of it. She kept trying to catch a glimpse of the fairies who might be flitting by, but the butterflies, bees, flies, and other insects kept distracting her.

There was so much to watch! So many flying creatures she wanted to chase! It was all so unfair that she was stuck here, babysitting her elder sister.

Then again, maybe turn-about was fair play. Angelina certainly had complained more than once about all the times she'd been stuck babysitting Merilee.

Finally, the fountain was clean, the water sparkling. Merilee could hear the difference in the tone of the splashes, how the water more closely resembled laughter.

"There," Angelina said, rolling her gloves off. She glanced over at Merilee. "Now what?"

The sun hadn't quite reached the high part of the sky, so it was still before noon.

Not that cat magic was tied to anything as mundane as a human clock.

Still, it wasn't quite the right time yet. The sun needed to be tickling the grass up here.

Merilee led Angelina back down the hill, back to the house, making her get into the shower and clean up. She'd be taking another shower later. This one was just to help prepare herself. Merilee rejected all of Angelina's shampoos, insisting that her sister use an unscented soap.

Really, did all humans seek to cover their scents so much?

Finally, when Angelina was clean to Merilee's standards, Merilee led her sister back up to the top of the hill.

Ah, the sun now filled the entire area. This was good.

While Merilee would have just liked to stretch out and bask in the sunshine for a while, she got right to work instead.

Angelina laid down on a towel, wearing a short-sleeved shirt and shorts. Her feet were bare, and her hair was still wet.

Merilee started with Angelina's right hand, licking the palm clean before moving to the back of the hand. She moved in regular, steady motion, purring softly as she did.

As she worked, she saw little wisps of smoke rise up out of Angelina's skin. Frequently, goosebumps crawled over her sister's skin in response.

Good. It was working.

It was going to take some time, but Merilee had all day.

CHAPTER 21

At first, Angelina seemed restless while being given her cat bath, particularly as the amount of smoke being released from her skin increased. Eventually, though, she relaxed, and appeared to be in a dream state by the time Merilee was finished.

Angelina sat up slowly, her eyes unfocused, her breathing deep and even. Merilee could tell that she was relaxed all the way to her bones. How long had it been since her sister had taken the time to breathe deeply?

Years, probably.

At Merilee's prompting, Angelina stood and walked over to the fairy fountain.

Though Merilee still didn't see any fairies, she did feel the presence of *something* there. It wasn't friendly, but it wasn't actively unfriendly either.

Hopefully, whatever it was would help.

After another push, Angelina reluctantly knelt down beside the fountain, cupped her hand, then drew water all along one arm. She gasped as the cold water touched her sun-warmed skin.

Merilee could tell it was working. It was as if there was a shadow Angelina stepping out from under her sister's skin, slowly working its way out.

The cat bath—roughening up her skin, opening her pores—had been the first step. Pouring blessed (blessed?) water on her skin was the second part.

Curious, Merilee stood on her hind legs, leaning against the edge of the fountain, looking into the basin.

She still couldn't see anything, so she cautiously reached down a paw, tapping the water.

Cold shot through her bones, but it was a good kind of chill. The kind that came from a brisk winter morning, when the sky would turn that remarkable shade of blue and the wind blew clear from the mountains.

Merilee shook herself. Yes, this would do the trick.

However, there was still one more thing for Angelina to do. Some trial for her to pass.

Merilee had the image of two kittens, playing. They'd rear up on hind paws, swatting at each other. One would fall over, then the other. They'd grapple for a few moments, until one yielded. Then they did it all over again.

It took Merilee a few moments to recognize the pattern.

Neither one was always on top. They took turns. Shared. Learned what it was like to be both the aggressor and the victim.

She cast a long glance at Angelina, who'd always been on top, as it were. Always been superior. The one with the best magic, the best grades, the cutest boyfriends. The one who everybody in the family always looked up to. She would take Mom's place someday as the head of the entire family. None of the other aunts or cousins were up for the job.

Angelina needed to learn how to give in once in a while.

But how could Merilee teach Angelina this? She couldn't turn Angelina into a cat, though that sounded like marvelous fun. Transformations weren't right. Angelina needed to stay human through this, so the lessons would be more applicable.

What else was up here? They were on the top tier of the garden. The second tier, below them, held a circle of rocks. Angelina, Merilee, and the other witches in their family used it for dancing, particularly on the solstice.

The bottom of the garden held patio furniture for those very, very few occasions when Angelina sat outside (Merilee could tell by how forlorn the chairs looked). Plus some beautiful plants, well-tended by the crew that Angelina hired to take care of the yard (something else that might have to change someday).

Merilee knew that Angelina couldn't just walk back down the hill. She had to do something else. Walk backwards? Slide, maybe?

It took Merilee a few more moments to figure it out.

Somersaults.

As kids, they'd had somersaulting contests. It was one thing that Merilee was actually better at than Angelina. Maybe she'd been born with the knowledge of how to turn things around, to move from the bottom to the top and back again.

She gave a healthy cat grin to Angelina, who, to her credit, seemed to understand that there was something up.

"Now what?" she asked. She sounded exasperated, but not seriously so. No, she had a twinkle in her eye that had been missing for quite some time now.

Merilee deliberately walked in a circle, carefully placing one paw after another. Then she looked expectantly at Angelina.

"Circles?" Angelina guessed.

Merilee nodded. Now, as a cat, it wasn't going to be easy to do a somersault. She just wasn't really built for that kind of thing. And she really wasn't a kitten, all twisty and made of springs.

Still, she gave it a try, throwing herself on her shoulder and rolling over.

Ow.

"What are you trying to do?" Angelina said, sounding more amused than frustrated.

Merilee tried again.

That wasn't going to work.

Instead, she laid down, and then rolled from one side to the other.

Finally, Angelina caught a clue.

"Somersaults? Like when we were kids?"

"Mrrow!" Merilee said, glad that Angelina had finally figured it out.

"No," Angelina said.

Huh. Merilee hadn't expected that level of vehemence.

She walked closer to Angelina.

"I'll get dirty!" Angelina said.

Merilee sat, waiting patiently, until Angelina got to the end of her excuses.

"And it's uncomfortable. And…what if someone sees?"

Merilee looked around the garden. Trees grew in abundance on either side. No one could easily peer into the backyard. They'd done that on purpose, encouraging the trees to grow so that the witches could have some privacy when they danced.

"Oh, goddess, I suppose you're right," Angelina said. She still sat for a moment, thinking.

"Doing somersaults down the hill, in my own backyard, shouldn't bother me in the least," she mused after a while. "There's something in me, though, something that's convinced I'll break something if I even try."

Was it the remnants of the dark magic? Bullies couldn't

bear to be laughed at. Richard was sure to be insulted by being called Dick. Angelina needed to get over herself if she wanted to heal.

Merilee butted her head against her sister's bare leg. Then she sat back and stared hard into Angelina's eyes.

Do it.

"It's just a little black magic," Angelina said after a few moments. "It can't be that bad, can it?" Then she shook her head, looking horrified. "I can't believe I just said that."

Angelina determinedly stood and walked to the edge of the hill. Then she paused, swaying.

"Why is this so ridiculously hard? It shouldn't be, should it?" she turned her head and looked over at Merilee for confirmation.

Merilee gave her a cat shrug. No, it shouldn't be that difficult to do.

However, the Great Angelina needed to let go. Or she'd never be fully clean.

"Here goes nothing," Angelina said. She squatted down, balancing on her toes. She stayed there for so long Merilee was thinking that she'd have to get up and push her sister to take that last step.

Finally, though, Angelina tucked herself in, folded further down on herself, and did her first somersault down the hill.

She paused after she finished, working her jaw. "I don't understand why I'm doing this," she complained bitterly.

Her body appeared to remember, though. She did a second summersault, then a third. She started giggling.

By the time she reached the bottom of the hill, Angelina was laughing madly. Merilee hurried after her. Had her sister broken something?

Even though she was now on flat ground, Angelina continued to do somersaults around the garden. Merilee watched, confused. She didn't smell anything wrong. Her sister's scent hadn't turned sour. If anything, it was sweeter now. More…human. Less chemical.

Finally, Angelina stopped. She had grass in her hair. Her shirt had mud stains along the spine. She threw out her arms and legs and giggled a bit more, looking like a dork.

Or perhaps a baby.

When she stopped laughing and pulled herself more together, she had a huge grin on her face.

"Thank you," she said. "I haven't felt so good, so light-hearted, in ages." She looked down at her feet. A blade of grass had gotten caught between her toes. She looked more pensive as she plucked it out. "The dark magic isn't as natural, is it?" she said, glancing over at Merilee.

Merilee shook her head. No, it was not.

"It's gone now," Angelina said, drawing in a deep breath and then releasing it.

Merilee didn't contradict her sister, though she knew that wasn't the full truth.

Her sister's dark magic was only gone for now.

CHAPTER 22

After a shower, lunch, and a nice nap, Angelina and Merilee sat together again in the eating nook, trying to come up with a plan for dealing with the first thug, Thing Two.

As he'd been the one who Angelina had actually met, he was the easiest for her to find. The other two might be a little more tricky, but hopefully Thing Two would be able to give them some clues as to their whereabouts.

Angelina used a scrying spell to figure out where Thing Two lived. She tied a small, enchanted magnet to a string, then gotten a map of Rochester and spread it out over the table. After she said a simple incantation, the magnet pulled against the string, leading them straight to the trailer park that was just south of town.

"Tornado magnet," Angelina said disdainfully when she realized the location.

Merilee sniffed. It wasn't that bad of a place. She'd gone to a couple of parties there when she'd been younger (and admittedly a bit more wild).

She then walked over and deliberately nuzzled against

Angelina, making sure that her scent was still pure and clean, that she hadn't accidentally dipped into any darker magic. But her sister still smelled of herself, and that mint soap that she was now going to favor (at Merilee's insistence).

"I didn't rejoin the dark side," Angelina said, scratching the top of Merilee's head.

Merilee sat down, with her butt on the cold table and her tail wrapped elegantly over her paws. She knew that it was the equivalent of a human raising one eyebrow in question.

Angelina appeared to read her expression correctly. "I didn't!" she said. "I mean, it's nice that you're worried about me and everything, but I'll be fine. I won't backslide. I promise."

Merilee flicked her tail back and forth a couple of times, the equivalent of a kitty shrug. Angelina didn't seem to catch that, though.

"Want to go get a bad guy?" Angelina said after a few moments. She turned to Merilee with a big grin. "I have an idea."

Merilee was pretty sure she wasn't going to like it. However, she'd at least listen to Angelina regarding it.

"There's this spell I know…it isn't bad," Angelina assured Merilee. "It's basically a transformation spell. How do you feel about changing into a tiger?"

Merilee considered it for a few moments. It didn't rub her fur the wrong way, but it didn't stroke it well either.

"Mrrow?" Merilee finally asked. *Why?*

"Thing Two is going to be the easiest of the three thugs. I'm hoping we can just scare him away," she explained.

Merilee considered her current form. She had longish white hair and green eyes. Six toes on the front paws and five on the back. The fur continued all the way down her legs and covered her paws.

She looked up and caught Angelina's eye, saying a single word.

Lynx.

Angelina broke into a huge smile. "I think that would work just fine."

CHAPTER 23

Merilee wasn't sure how she'd feel traveling in Angelina's car. Turned out, it wasn't a problem. She'd driven school buses for the past few years. It had been an easy, pretty mindless job that gave her a lot of time off for pursuing other things, like cooking or gardening, things that witches were supposedly good at but that she'd always struggled with.

Being in a car while she was still house-cat sized was a lot like being in a bus, with the same sort of proportions. She roamed across the back seat of Angelina's white Lexus, going from one window to the other, standing up on her rear legs so she could see out.

All right, so possibly she was spreading her fur as much as she possibly could in her sister's too-perfect car.

And really, it was *not* her fault when Angelina abruptly braked and Merilee ended up digging her claws into the leather of the seat.

Angelina merely glared at Merilee for it, and didn't say anything.

Maybe the somersaults had relaxed her sister some,

cranked down her too-tightly-wound nature. It would take some time for her to get fully relaxed. Hopefully not too long.

They parked the car on the street outside the trailer park. It was far too nice of a car for this neighborhood, and it would be remembered.

Merilee didn't suggest that Angelina rub some dirt into the car or anything. That might have been a step too far, at least at this point.

Instead, they made their way by foot through the trailer park. It was hard for Merilee to tell if the place had changed much. It had been so many years ago since she'd last been here. Plus before, she'd come here at night. Also, her perspective was completely different now. Instead of looking at the trailer homes, she was looking at the bushes, the cracks in the concrete sidewalks, the leaves that were already covered in dust.

There was less of the omnipresent human smell here. The back of the trailer park opened up onto woods. The smell of the trees snuck in between all the other scents, along with the smell of a nearby artificial lakes.

Merilee couldn't help but shiver being close to a large body of water. That was how she'd died the first time.

She really didn't want to die again, particularly by drowning.

Angelina's magnet led them to the residence of Thing Two. Seemed the thug lived in a single-wide trailer that had seen better days. Rotting latticework covered the base of it. The trailer itself had once been white with blue trim around the windows and door, but was now dingy. The siding was pulling off, and it was rusted underneath. Merilee wrinkled her nose at the smell of mildew and putrid earth.

Sheets covered the windows, not allowing in any light. A big "No Soliciting" sign hung next to the door.

"We aren't soliciting anything, are we?" Angelina asked innocently enough.

Merilee twitched her tail. Nope. They were just looking for Thing Two to leave. Now.

The pair of them walked up the steps, Angelina with spells in hand, and Merilee ready to leap in.

They didn't bother knocking. After waving her hand over the door, Angelina pushed it open.

"What are you do—" Thing Two started to say. He was sitting on a ratty couch, drinking a can of beer, wearing a pair of navy-blue board shorts and no shirt.

The smell of unwashed human filled Merilee's nose. The awful shag carpet that had seen better days crunched under her paws as she walked in.

Merilee felt herself change as she walked across the room. In the time it took for her to take three steps, she'd tripled in size. Instead of being a good-sized housecat, she was now the size of a large German Shepard, over one hundred pounds and still growing.

She'd maintained her white fur, a good long coat of it. The ruff around her face had elongated, with the classic black points of a "bow tie" at her neck. Her paws were huge, larger than a human's hand. She did regret that her tail abruptly shrank, down to just a stub. A loud, deep growl rumbled out of her chest.

Before Thing Two could say or do anything, Merilee pounced on him. She kept her claws sheathed—she wouldn't do the thug damage unless she had to.

Merilee would have the opportunity to "play" later if he didn't cooperate.

Thing Two sank back against the couch and Merilee panted directly into his face, her front paws holding his arms to the side, her back paws digging into his thighs.

"Do I have your attention now?" Angelina said from the side.

The human underneath Merilee tensed, as if he was going to try something stupid like get up and fling her away.

Tsk. Tsk.

Merilee let just the tips of her claws come out to pin him down more firmly. She stared down at him. Her eyes were still green, Angelina had told her they didn't change, no matter what form she took. It was strange, as her human form had had brown eyes. Kind of plain, honestly.

She hoped she looked hungry. Or hungry enough. She growled again as he shifted.

Thing Two finally froze.

"You won't get away with this," Thing Two said, trying for bravado.

"Get away with what?" Angelina asked. She sounded as though she couldn't be bothered, and was just asking out of politeness.

"Killing me," he said.

"You aren't worth killing," Angelina said coolly.

Merilee whined and licked her chops hungrily.

"Fine, possibly you could become cat food, but honestly? I wouldn't trust where that meat has been," Angelina pointed out.

Merilee tilted her head to the side and stared at Thing Two. She went back to the growl, as if to say that she didn't care.

"We're not here for you. We have bigger fish to fry, as it were," Angelina continued. "Tell me where I can find your boss."

"Who, Mr. Keebler?" Thing Two asked, obviously confused.

"No, the other thugs who made the mistake of trying to

do harm to my sister," Angelina said. Now, she sounded pissed.

Merilee leaned forward, making an obvious show of sniffing at the neck of Thing Two. Oh, goddess. Gross. He hadn't seen a shower in a few days, and he'd been drinking heavily. Had he been trying to work up the courage to do something? Something even worse than drowning a harmless cat?

He shivered under her, the smell of fear overwhelming the rank body odor.

"Nialto? And Bennet?" Thing Two said, his voice cracking. "Sure. I don't have addresses for them. Just phone numbers."

Angelina lifted her hand. Wherever Thing Two's phone had been hiding, it unearthed itself and flew through the air to her hand.

It only took Angelina a few moments to ferret out the electronic information.

Merilee flexed her claws when Thing Two tensed again. Did he think that if Angelina was distracted that she would be as well? No, she had one job here, to scare him.

Though scaring someone wasn't really her forte. No, she was much better at *playing* with them.

She wondered if she could let Thing Two go. What it might be like to chase him. To pounce on him. Or would that be her own slippery slope to the darker magics?

Thoughts for another day.

"Got it," Angelina said. She dropped the phone onto the coffee table in front of the couch. It cracked ominously when it landed. "Now, what to do with you?"

"I'm nothing," Thing Two said. He had tensed before, thinking about making a run for it. Now, it was pure fear. "There isn't anything you have to do with me."

Merilee growled and opened her mouth, just brushing her teeth across his neck.

"No! Really! There isn't anything I know. Or can do," Thing Two said. "I don't know what they have planned for you. Except maybe to get the cat away from you," he added.

"I may have already figured that out," Angelina said. "Since you have already drowned poor Merilee's familiar."

"The boss said to take it, since we couldn't find her," Thing Two said hastily. "But we weren't going to harm your sister! We weren't supposed to do anything but grab her and hold on to her."

"I still don't approve of people who would drown a poor, defenseless cat," Angelina said.

Merilee added in her own growls and pressed down slightly with her teeth on the guy's throat.

"And neither does she," Angelina added, knowing that who she meant would be obvious.

"I get it. I get it!" Thing Two said.

More fear poured out of him. He actually started to shake, now.

Merilee almost felt bad for him.

Almost.

"But that still doesn't answer the question of what are we going to do with you," Angelina said. She walked over to stand in front of Thing Two. "What do you think, my dear. Hmmm?" Angelina stroked Merilee's back once, twice.

Merilee contained her kitty sigh. Instead, she obeyed their pre-arranged signal and hopped down, off of Thing Two's body. She may have accidentally scratched his thighs a bit. Nothing too bad. A little antiseptic and those scratches would clear right up.

She came to sit obediently at Angelina's side. She really wasn't obeying anyone but herself, though Thing Two would never know that.

"I think that you, leaving, now, today, would probably be the best thing for everyone," Angelina announced.

"What, leave? And go where?" Thing Two asked.

Merilee leaned slightly against Angelina. Thing Two did *not* have the resources that the pair of them did. If she wanted him to go, she was going to have to provide the means as well.

"I don't care," Angelina said. She reached into her bag, pulled out a wad of cash, and dropped it negligently on the coffee table. "Go wherever you want. Just don't stay here. Or else."

"Or else what?" Thing Two asked. His entire attention was focused on the cash, one hand already starting to slowly reach for it.

"Or else kitty is going to come back to play. Isn't that right, kitty?" Angelina asked, tousling the hair on Merilee's head.

The growl Merilee gave was heartfelt. Not so much for Thing Two's sake, but because she *really* didn't like anyone rubbing her fur the wrong way.

"I get it," Thing Two said, suddenly scooting all the way back on the couch again.

"And don't let anyone, in particular, Nialto or Bennet, know that you're going anywhere. You shouldn't call them until after you arrive somewhere else," Angelina specified.

Merilee gave another growl, followed by a suddenly leap. She landed on the couch next to Thing Two, continuing to growl, advancing slowly on him.

"I'll go. I promise!" Thing Two said, backing away as far as he could. "I won't tell anyone!"

Merilee raised one fur-covered paw and bopped him on the nose.

Thing Two squealed loudly. "I'll go!"

"Good," Angelina said.

Merilee raised her head. The smell of smoke had just entered the room. Was that from one of the neighbors? Or was Thing Two's lunch burning on the stove?

She didn't have a tail to twitch, not really. She still gave as close as she could to a feline shrug.

"We'll see ourselves out," Angelina said. "Come on, kitty."

Merilee gave one last good growl in Thing Two's direction, before she leaped off the couch, following after Angelina toward the door.

Wait. Where was that smoke coming from?

The wall behind the TV had started to glow. The distinct taste of ashes filled Merilee's mouth.

Crap. There was another incendiary amulet imbedded there.

Had someone been listening in on their conversation? Or was it just Angelina's presence that had triggered it?

"Rrrrooowww!" Merilee yelled.

Angelina had already opened the door, but had paused to look back.

Merilee took a mighty leap and butted her head against Angelina's legs, knocking her free of the trailer.

Then she turned back, intending to haul Thing Two out of the trailer next.

Too late.

The explosion lifted her up. She felt her back crushed against the ceiling. White hot fire chased across her fur, then dove deep into her bones. Cackling fire surrounded her.

She yowled in anguish.

Then all was dark.

~

Merilee opened her eyes. She was still in the trailer, though it was empty. The portal blazed blue on the threshold of the open door.

What would happen if she didn't walk through it? Merilee turned her head to look around.

The rest of the room faded, growing dim and full of shadows.

Oh.

She could either go through the portal, or she could stay here, and become a ghost. She'd be trapped here, in the location she died in.

That wouldn't be fun.

What had happened to Angelina? Back in the real world? Had Merilee saved her?

She didn't know. But she had to get back there. Had to find out.

Merilee crouched, then made a running leap for the portal.

Going faster didn't appear to help.

What breath she'd had at some point now caught in her lungs, burning. Her paws were on fire. Tears dripped down from her face. The tips of her ears were singed. Even her nose burned. It was awful. Every single step.

Was it always the same number of steps? To get through the portal? It must be.

She hated every single moment of it. The way the portal grabbed hold of her fur, tugging out pieces of it. How weak she felt as she made her way. The pain—honestly, the pain wasn't the worst of it. No, there was heartbreak as well, the sense of dragging her soul across a burning valley, bruising her paws with every step.

Finally, Merilee reached the end of it and stepped out.

Again, the blissful light waited for her. It had moved

considerably closer this time. It wouldn't take much, just a step, maybe two, and she could rest in peace finally.

Not yet. Not until she'd actually saved her sister.

Merilee stubbornly turned toward the other light. It had an orange glow this time. She assumed that meant more fire that way as well.

With a put-upon kitty sigh, Merilee stepped through, returning to the land of the living.

One more time.

LIFE FIVE

Merilee didn't see fire when she opened her eyes. No, instead she saw the dashboard of the Lexus.

It appeared that Angelina had scooped up her body and carried her to the car, laying her on the front seat.

Merilee gave a soft groan as she stretched, her back feeling scrunched together. Being blown against the ceiling had kind of stuck with her this time.

"You're awake?" Angelina asked. She reached out a hand and for the first time, scritched Merilee just right along her jaw line. "Are you okay?"

Merilee shook herself and stretched some more. No, she wasn't okay. She was certain that her beautiful, luxurious fur had diminished. It wasn't scraggly, not yet, but it would be. The toe beans on her footpads were no longer pink and soft, but had changed to a darker color, and were cracked. Her claws, too, weren't as white. A few of them had yellowed significantly. She knew if she wasn't careful using them, they'd crack and splinter.

"Mrrrow," Merilee said after a few moments. She gave a

soft sigh as she forced herself to stand up and look at Angelina who sat in the driver's seat.

"I know," Angelina said. "I'm sorry I didn't even know his name," she said after a few moments. She turned to look at Merilee. "Do you know what caused the explosion?"

Another firetruck came whining toward the trailer park.

Merilee nodded and stared hard into Angelina's eyes.

Amulet. In wall.

"There was an amulet in the trailer? Imbedded in the wall?" Angelina said, shocked. "Why? Who would do that?"

"Mrrow," Merilee replied. She didn't know. Perhaps it had been one of the other thugs. Probably the same person who had placed the amulet in the rear wheel well of Angelina's car.

"And, what, it went off in my presence?" Angelina continued.

Again, Merilee didn't know for certain, but that certainly would have been her guess.

"Someone is really out to get me," Angelina said, looking away from Merilee, staring out of the front window of the car while she thought.

"Look, I know you're tired. I'm tired too," she said. "But we're going to need to confront the other two thugs tonight."

Merilee wanted to yowl in response. Angelina had no idea how tired she was, how much effort it took to drag herself back to life every time. Faint memories of the pain made her paws tingle and her nose twitch.

But if whoever had placed those amulets was willing to kill, Angelina and Merilee had to keep moving.

"I'm going to set up a meeting with Nialto and Bennet," Angelina told her.

Merilee nodded and dropped back down onto the seat. Angelina turned the car on and pressed a button.

Glorious warmth sprang up from the seat. Oh, this was heaven. Merilee had forgotten that Angelina's car had seat warmers up front.

She purred and stretched out, letting the seat absorb whatever cold had remained from her last death. She may have even fallen asleep. It wasn't until she realized that the car had stopped moving, that it had been moving, that she opened her eyes again.

"Mrrow?" she inquired, standing and stretching.

"Nialto and Bennet are meeting us at the wastewater reclamation plant," Angelina told her.

Merilee gave a deep kitty sigh at the news. Of course. They'd want to meet near water. Someplace that they believed would put them at an advantage.

"I won't let them drown you again," Angelina said firmly.

Merilee couldn't help but roll her eyes at that. Her sister wouldn't be able to protect her. She knew that, deep in her bones. No, Merilee just had to make certain that the thugs couldn't catch her.

How had Angelina gotten Nialto and Bennet to agree to meet with her at all? What had she promised them? Merilee wasn't certain she wanted to know. Particularly not given the slightly sour smell of her sister.

Merilee leaped over the armrest between the seats, landing in Angelina's lap. It wasn't that comfortable, not with the steering wheel right there. She licked at her sister's neck, chasing away the vinegary scent.

"All right. All right!" Angelina said after a few moments. She wrapped her hands around Merilee's torso and pulled her back. "I had to power the magic somehow," she said. The more familiar scent of her anger rose up.

"Mrrow," Merilee said. She didn't care. Angelina was

going to slide back if she wasn't more careful. She shoved her face forward again, licking Angelina's nose.

"I get it!" Angelina said. "Fine. I won't dip into the stronger stuff. Even if we need it."

Merilee sighed. She knew that as soon as push came to shove, Angelina would backslide.

Would it be more difficult to clean her a second time? Just as it was harder for Merilee to come back to life? Probably.

Merilee growled deep in her chest, so that Angelina could feel the rumble against her fingers more than she could hear it.

Angelina sighed. "You're right. I shouldn't have done it."

The sour smell started to dissipate.

Good. The Great Angelina needed to stay more humble, to remember her place, to not push so hard.

They'd get through this.

Merilee looked at her sister, then back at the other seat.

Angelina actually caught the hint and lifted Merilee over the armrest.

"Mrrow?" Merilee asked.

"What's the plan?" Angelina asked. She gave a bitter laugh. "Well, to start with, we tell them what happened to Thing Two. His name was Daryl, by the way."

That was good to know. Merilee nodded, encouraging Angelina to go on.

"They have to know that they're being set up by Richard. That they're completely expendable, as far as Richard is concerned," Angelina continued.

Dick the Elf Merilee corrected in her head.

"So it will be in their best interests to work for me, rather than to keep working for Richard," Angelina continued.

"Mrrow?" Merilee said. *That's it?*

Angelina gave Merilee a brilliant smile. "Plus, I have a

call scheduled to go in to the authorities to report trespassing on the site if they don't agree."

Merilee bobbed her head, giggling.

It wasn't the greatest plan. However, it was what they had given their general lack of preparation.

Hopefully, it would be enough.

CHAPTER 25

Merilee didn't need to read the signs directing them to the HPO—Higher Purity Oxygen—plant. She merely had to follow her nose.

The smells here weren't great. There was a lot of chlorine in the air, as well as the stench of sewer water. At least they weren't meeting in one of the sludge plants, which she assumed would be worse.

However, the purer oxygen content was obvious. As a human, she'd read about oxygen bars, how people got a real high from breathing purer air. As a cat, she could practically taste the cleaner air. Yes, it was carefully contained in tall cylinders scattered around the plant. There wasn't supposed to be any escaping. She could still smell it, though.

The problem was that the scents were very distracting. There weren't any mice in the plant, not that she could tell. Humans had been here, but the air kept their scent to a minimum.

No, it was that damned sewage that kept snagging her attention. It wasn't merely human waste, no. It was everything that someone might send through their garbage disposal, such as orange peels, coffee grounds, egg shells, kale stems, tomato skins, rose petals, and all the cleaning chemicals.

She suddenly realized the advantage the thugs had by meeting in a place such as this. She wouldn't be able to track either Nialto or Bennet via their scent. It would be very difficult to tease those smells out, apart from all the others.

Of course, she could do it. It would just take time, effort, and concentration. Things she surely wouldn't have a lot of.

Merilee stayed hidden in the shadows, near one of the working consoles. She liked the way the lights played across the board. It was very soothing. If she wasn't careful, it would hypnotize her, another distraction to take her eyes off the prize.

Damn it! She needed to focus.

There was a cold concrete floor under her tail and paws. It had been washed recently with a faux lemon chemical cleaner. The lights throughout the room had been turned down to low. The primary lighting came from the panel. Water whooshing through the tubes, swirling around the container in the center, sounded a little like the ocean. But it was too regular to be natural.

Angelina stood beside Merilee, checking her phone, of course. While Merilee understood the attraction, she also knew that it was yet another distraction. Angelina needed to be paying more attention!

Merilee shifted over and pressed one paw down on Angelina's foot. She might have put all her weight onto it.

"They're not here yet," Angelina murmured. "No one has come through the door."

Merilee gave an expressive kitty sigh.

She didn't need to use doors. Why did the thugs?

However, Angelina turned out to be right. After just a few moments, she put her phone away.

"They're here," she said. "They just walked through the door. They didn't notice the charm I had tied to it."

Merilee had to nod her approval. Fine. So Angelina was still better at magic than she was. At least some things.

Nialto and Bennet slipped into the room. Nialto turned out to be the boss, while Bennet was Thing One.

They were both dressed all in black again. Seriously, even cops wouldn't take anyone dressed that way seriously. They wore black cotton pants, black hoodies, and even black gloves.

"Hello?" Bennet called out.

"Shhhh," Nialto said.

Merilee couldn't help but snicker. Must be hell having to work with such poor minions.

Though their incompetence was why she was still alive.

"I'm right here," Angelina said, stepping out from the other side of the big basin of water.

Nialto glared at her across the way. Bennet stood still, trying to look tough.

Was that fear Merilee smelled on him? Possibly.

She stayed where she was, hidden in the shadows. She wasn't to leap out at them unless absolutely necessary.

She had no desire to lose yet another life. Her hips were already complaining about the cold floor. She wasn't sure how much she could rely on her claws, whether they'd scratch or she'd break them off.

Angelina hadn't brought the ingredients to load another lynx spell, so Merilee was stuck at her current size.

It would be more than enough. She was certain.

"Whatcha want?" Nialto said.

"You heard about Daryl, right?" Angelina asked innocently enough.

Nialto's eyes narrowed. "Yeah, we heard all right. You killed him. Blew up his place."

"I did *not* blow up his place," Angelina said. "Someone planted an incendiary device in the wall of his trailer. My presence there activated it."

"Oh," Nialto said, obviously taken back.

"You can bet that if I showed up at either of your places of residence, the same thing would happen," Angelina said. "Your boss is making sure that there aren't any loose tongues."

Nialto glanced over at Bennet, who shrugged. Their smell had changed from fear to determination.

At least as far as Merilee could surmise. It was awfully hard to tell for certain.

"So what?" Nialto said. "I've done worse to ensure loyalty in my crew."

Bennet shifted nervously at that.

Merilee wasn't sure if Nialto was bluffing. He wasn't a big-time criminal, she could tell that. Like Angelina, Nialto preferred to be the big fish in the small pond.

On the other hand, he was tougher than Bennet or Daryl. She'd bet that he'd served real time in prison, unlike the other two, who were small-time thugs.

"So you might want to consider a change of employer," Angelina said. "I can pay you better than Richard can. I will certainly give you better working hours and conditions."

"You wouldn't have any work for us," Nialto countered. "You're too much of a goody two-shoes. Naw, we'll stick with the agreement we already have."

"I was afraid of that," Angelina said. She held up her cell phone rather dramatically, and pressed a button.

An alarm suddenly blared out, breaking through the quiet sound of the slushing water.

"The police are on their way," Angelina announced. "I can hide you. Or you can face them."

"You really don't get it, do you, lady?" Nialto said.

Suddenly, there was a gun in his hand.

Crap! Merilee hadn't smelled it on him at all. Did it have some sort of camouflage spell on it? So that it couldn't be sensed?

"You don't scare me," Nialto continued. "You never scared me. Sure, you've got some power. Mr. Keebler's shown us, let us watch some of what you can do. But him…he's got a lot more. And a lot more connections in both high as well as low places. We can't just turn our backs on him. He'll do us in."

"Then you'll have to deal with the cops," Angelina said. She stepped to the side, a portal opening up behind her.

The smell in the room changed, going from determination to fearful anguish.

But it wasn't coming from Nialto.

No, Bennet was the one who was truly afraid.

It surprised Merilee how quickly Bennet moved, snatching the gun away from Nialto. His boss looked stunned, as if he'd never expected Bennet to turn that way.

"I can't go back to prison, boss," Bennet said as way of apology. "I can't. You know that."

"It's all right," Nialto said, trying to placate his armed and dangerously unstable minion. "Mr. Keebler will take care of us."

"Will he?" Bennet asked. "Or will he *take care of us*, the same way he took care of Daryl?"

Nialto didn't appear to have a good answer for that.

"The only way, the *only way* Mr. Keebler will help us out is if we help him out," Bennet continued. He turned the gun away from Nialto and now focused it on Angelina. "You know that he's run out of patience with this one."

"He don't want her killed," Nialto warned.

Bennet shrugged. "He wouldn't mind it," he said. "You know what we placed in her car."

Great. So he was admitting to putting the amulet in the rear wheel well. It would have exploded at some point, killing Angelina.

Nialto glared at Bennet, clearly telling his armed minion to keep his mouth shut.

"We've already found that lovely amulet," Angelina said. "And destroyed it."

Bennet kept the gun pointed stock still at Angelina, while at the same time glanced around the rest of the control room. "You have a familiar here somewhere," he ground out. "I don't have the magic of these others. But I can still smell cat in here. Call her out."

"Now, why would I bring my familiar here?" Angelina said. "I don't need her."

Bennet gave a deprecating laugh. "You wouldn't risk leaving her at home." He peered at Angelina. "You know it isn't safe there."

Merilee bristled at that. Was there something her sister was hiding from her? Or had they already cleared out all the danger, like the protection spells around the house, and all the bad ingredients above the fridge?

"It's far safer there than here," Angelina said. She wisely stayed where she was, not making a move toward the portal.

While Merilee figured that Angelina could move quickly if she needed to, she couldn't outrun a bullet. Any more than Merilee could.

"Why don't we find out for sure?" Bennet said casually.

The sound of the gunshot hurt Merilee's ears. She yowled in displeasure and leaped out of her shadow, racing toward Angelina.

That asshole hadn't hurt her, had he?

Angelina still stood soundly in place. Merilee didn't smell blood over the sudden scent of the gunpowder.

"Ah, there she is," Bennet said. He aimed casually for Merilee.

Merilee dashed to the side, narrowly avoiding the madman's bullet.

"What are you doing?" Nialto said.

Wailing sirens sounded in the distance.

"I told you. I can't go back to prison," Bennet explained gently. He sounded as if he were being very patient, explaining everything to a young child. "You know that."

"Look, Mr. Keebler—"

"Can't count on him. Can't count on you, either," Bennet said.

He almost sounded sad as he shot his boss.

"What are you doing?" Angelina said. "Stop that!"

Bennet shrugged. "Death by cop. Ain't the worst thing in the world. Now, if I can only take you with me, that will convince them to shoot first, ask questions later."

The world slowed down as Bennet aimed. Angelina had a spell ready, but Merilee could tell that she wouldn't get it off in time.

She only meant to distract the madman. To draw his attention away from her sister. To give her the time she needed to protect herself.

She hadn't meant to get herself shot. And killed. Again.

Merilee didn't take any time with regrets. Didn't pause for even a moment. She barely took in her surroundings—still in the control room for the HPO plant—before she passed through the gray portal.

She had to get back as quickly as possible. Angelina was in danger.

Bennet was too much of a coward to merely turn the gun on himself. No, he needed to take everyone with him.

Damn him!

The pain took what little breath Merilee had in her lungs away. Her gut ached this time—probably where she'd been shot. Great. Now she was going to have stomach issues. She just knew it.

Would serve Angelina right if Merilee made sure to throw up in her shoes every time.

The way the portal pulled at her fur let her know that it was going to show more, once she came back to life. She didn't think she was too vain as a cat, but she was a little proud of how luxurious her fur felt.

Used to feel.

Instead of extreme heat or cold, this time, Merilee felt waterlogged, as if a great weight was pulling her down, holding her back. She struggled as she passed through the portal, trying to maintain her speed, to rush through as quickly as possible.

It was almost as if something were holding her back.

Was it because the place where she was returning to wasn't safe? Too bad. She still needed to get back. Now.

As she expected, the bright warm patch of light leading to the blissful place was closer than ever. She knew that in a few (just a few!) more lives, it would appear right under the portal, and she wouldn't be able to escape it, wouldn't be able to look away.

She'd die completely, at that point.

No, she had work to do.

Merilee firmly turned away from that light and walked into the dark patch that felt cold to her, colder than sunless concrete.

If Bennet hadn't already died, she was going to make him pay for this.

LIFE SIX

Merilee was surprised to find herself lying on the floor of the HPO control room. Surely Angelina would have picked her up and taken her away when she left? Had she managed to return that quickly? While the action was still going on?

The sound of a gunshot echoed loudly through the room, making Merilee jump to her feet and yowl.

Several things happened at the same time.

Three policemen in full riot gear stood at the doorway, their weapons drawn and firing. They weren't carefully shooting, no, they were spraying the room with bullets.

Bennet started to fall like a dead leaf from a tree, slowly tumbling over and to the side.

Shouts echoed over and under the sounds of the battle and the constant bangs from the guns.

Why were the cops still shooting the body? Were they afraid that Bennet would rise back up?

Merilee yowled again.

One of the cops flinched, jerking his gun in her direction.

Oh no.

She didn't have time to run away. To even flick her tail once.

Then she was dead. Again.

Of course they'd shot her.

She'd appeared as a black cat, not as a white one.

~

This time, Merilee took her time going before she approached the portal, letting colors bleed out of the control room, take on a more ghostly appearance.

It would drive her crazy to be stuck here, haunting this plant for the rest of her existence. She wasn't certain how she'd be able to leave. There had to be a way. It seemed unfair to be trapped here, in such a place.

Now, if it were a cozy home that she was used to, with marvelous sunbeams to lie in and all the good sniffs, she could see being tempted.

Eventually, Merilee gathered up her courage and pushed herself through the portal.

Again, there was this water-logged feeling. If she still had a beating heart, it would be pounding madly in her chest.

This was too similar to the first time she'd died, when she'd drown.

Her lungs were burning. Her gut, too. Her paws flailed against nothing. She didn't feel as though she was making any progress.

She couldn't get stuck here, could she?

But then came the too-familiar feeling of her fur being pulled out by the roots.

Damn it! She was really going to miss that fur. She was likely to feel the cold much more now. It was going to sink into her bones and stay there.

Maybe she could get Angelina to buy her a heated mat or pillow or something.

If she ever had a chance to rest. Which she doubted.

They'd taken care of the three thugs. They weren't going to come after either Angelina or Merilee again.

However, now they had to face *Dick the Elf.*

And he wasn't likely to play fair.

Merilee gave one last push, finally reaching the end of the portal, stepping out on the far side. At least she was still in the HPO control room.

The calm light to the side entranced her. It was difficult to look away. It filled her with the sense of longing.

It would be so lovely to step into that light. To leave the world and all its struggles.

As she watched, the light moved temptingly closer.

But no. She had a sister to take care of. Angelina would never survive the coming conflict without her.

Oh, she might survive Dick. But she'd probably also return to the dark side, and lose herself.

Nope. Angelina needed her.

So Merilee walked past the comforting light, back into the darkness, one more time.

LIFE SEVEN

At least this time when Merilee woke up, she was back in the car with Angelina. The salty smell of her sister's tears brought her no joy.

"Mrrow?" she asked softly.

Goddess, this time she *hurt*. It was as if her ribs were still bruised. Her gut rolled uncomfortably. She wasn't sure if she needed to poop or to vomit. Or maybe both. Thick scum covered her teeth, as if she hadn't eaten anything solid in days. Pain made her head throb, as if her skull were too small for her brain.

Maybe it was. She felt as though she'd shrunken this time, gone from being a healthy-sized house cat to something smaller. Older. More frail.

"I'm sorry, I'm so sorry, I'm so, so sorry," Angelina said, running her fingers over Merilee's side gently. "That hurt. I know. It must have really hurt this time."

"Mrrow," Merilee said. She tried to push herself up, but kind of failed, and instead, after a few moments, lay back down.

It was only then that she felt the heat from the seats warming her back and side. She stretched into it, relaxing.

"We've got to go now," Angelina said softly. "Get you back home. Get us a little breathing space."

Merilee merely nuzzled her head against Angelina's hand for a few moments before she let herself fall into a dark, blissful sleep.

She awoke curled up on the pillow she'd slept on before, on Angelina's couch. She must have really been sleeping hard, if Angelina could pick her up and move her without her waking at all.

At least she finally felt better. Slower, sure. Her joints were bothering her, even in her sleep. She ran her tongue across her teeth before she yawned. Yeah, she was going to have problems with them soon as well.

Merilee got up off the pillow onto the more stable couch cushions (and since when had it bothered her to be on an unstable surface?). She stretched more, spending time moving all her joints around, getting the blood back flowing into every part of her.

Then, just because she could, she leaped off the couch and raced from there to the front door. She spun after she reached there, dislodging the front mat, then ran back, bounding over the couch, onto the coffee table, from one chair to the next, before racing away again.

It felt so good to get her heart pounding, to stretch her legs and race, not because she was running in fear.

Finally, Merilee's stomach told her to stop. It rumbled loudly enough she figured that Angelina could probably hear it.

What was there to eat?

She paused for a moment, checking her internal clock. The birds had only just awoken and were serenading each other, which meant that by human time, it was about 4 AM.

Hopefully, Angelina had left something for Merilee. Otherwise, there was going to be tuna juice on the kitchen floor. Again.

And yet, Merilee wasn't sure that she wanted tuna. Actually, some of that chicken she'd had before sounded like it would be much more tasty at this time. And that was in the fridge.

Merilee sauntered confidently into the kitchen area. What could she find today?

She sat in front of the refrigerator, staring hard at it. How did her magic work? Could she open the fridge? She couldn't really push it open from the side. She didn't have the strength.

Maybe she'd have to get Angelina to rig up a belt or a rope or something, that Merilee could tug on to open the door.

Problems for later.

For now, Merilee stared at the closed door and meditated on what to do. Finally, it occurred to her that she'd fallen into her old human habits.

Cat magic wasn't done standing still. No, she had to *move*.

Merilee started pacing in a tight circle. She added a low growl, deep in her throat. The white-painted wooden cabinets echoed the sound softly. Her claws clicked against the cool tile floor. The smell of something natural, like a fresh breeze from across green fields, swirled through the area.

Finally, the door of the refrigerator slowly opened.

Merilee spotted the dish she remembered from before, the one filled with chicken. Luckily, it was on a lower shelf.

The refrigerator section was at the top of the appliance. The bottom was a freezer compartment, a drawer that pulled out. Merilee was able to leap up and sit on the top of the freezer door while reaching with her paw for the container.

It didn't take much maneuvering to get the dish off the shelf, sliding it out and then letting it fall.

She appeared to be lucky that morning! The lid bounced off as the container hit the floor.

Merilee jumped down, unable to contain the grunt of pain that flared in her now arthritic hips. Maybe there was something she could take for that. Or perhaps there was some sort of cat magic she could figure out, to help.

She knew that warmth would be good, too. She planned on spending at least part of the day looking out the various windows of Angelina's house, finding the best sunbeams and sleeping.

She needed the rest. Hopefully Angelina did too, and they could take a day or more before they made their next move.

Merilee finished eating, then jumped back up to poke her nose into the fridge. What else did Angelina have that might be edible?

There was the soy milk, which wasn't milk at all.

Merilee thought for a moment, then "accidentally" knocked it over, spilling it down the side of the fridge.

Oops.

The vegetables in the drawer didn't interest her in the least. Nor did the herbs, half of which she knew were used both in spells as well as in cooking. She wasn't going to bother those, as they tended to be harmless.

But there was something here. She kept poking around, shifting things from one side to the other.

Leftover take-out Chinese? Nope. Too much soy.

Oatmeal? Yuck. Difficult to identify, because it was so bland.

The eggs she was careful about. She liked eggs, both as a human as well as a cat.

Though bacon didn't interest her, she was careful with it as well.

Finally, in the far back corner on the second shelf, Merilee snagged a strand of something. It looked as though it had once been a flower stem, though the petals were now all withered. She was about to take it in her mouth but paused.

There was something not right with it.

Why had Bennet said that Angelina's house wasn't safe? Was it because her sister had things hidden here and there? Things that Merilee wouldn't find on her first pass through the house, cleaning up the darker spell ingredients? Or was there something else?

It took some doing, but Merilee finally managed to pull the long stem out of the fridge without ever either using her mouth or sinking a claw into it. She deliberately stepped into the puddle of soy milk on the floor, a few times, using it as water to wash her paws clean before turning back to the stem.

She finally recognized what it was—an old stalk of Foxglove.

Sure, it had its uses, even for good witches. Merilee knew a couple of healing spells that used it. However, Angelina was no healer.

Merilee was certain that plenty of dark magic would use such an ingredient. The plant was both poisonous and toxic, that is, its leaves could cause a rash, and ingesting it could kill a person.

How many other spell ingredients did Angelina have hidden around the house that Merilee had missed her first time?

"What are you doing?" Angelina screeched from the side of the kitchen. "What did you spill?"

"Mrrow," Merilee said in reply. Not really an answer. Just sort of a, "Yeah, so?"

"I can't believe you," Angelina said exasperated. "You could have waited until I was awake. Or woken me up. I would have gotten up to feed you. I owe you, you know."

Merilee sat with her head tilted to one side. She felt a little bad. Not a lot. But a little.

She was so used to the Mighty Angelina that she hadn't tried to give her sister a chance. It had never even occurred to her that her sister might feel indebted.

A week before, Angelina probably would never have admitted to such an emotion.

Now, it felt kind of cool.

"Mrrow," Merilee said. *Sorry.*

She waited while Angelina finished fussing and cleaning up the spilled soy. (She refused to call it *milk*. Whatever it was, it wasn't that.) As well as picked up what was left of the chicken. Angelina glanced at the container, then back at Merilee. "This is yours, now," she said firmly. "I'm not eating the rest of it."

Merilee flicked her tail as a shrug. She might. She might not. It would depend on what her stomach guided her to eat next.

When Angelina appeared to be finished, Merilee *mrrowed* loudly, getting her attention.

"Yes?" Angelina said with a sigh.

Merilee stepped to the side to reveal the long Foxglove stem.

Angelina saw it, blinked, then sighed. "Yeah, okay. I missed that one. But so did you," she added hastily. "I'll toss it. With the rest of the ingredients."

Merilee caught the odd phrasing of Angelina's. Hadn't she already thrown out all those other ingredients? She'd seen her sister put them all in a garbage bag. Where was that bag now?

Merilee ignored Angelina's attempt at getting her

attention and instead, concentrated on sniffing the air, scenting for that bag.

She walked to the back door, looked at Angelina, then back to the door.

"What, you want to go out? We're going to have to get you a cat door or something," Angelina complained. But she opened the door.

There, sitting right beside it, was the bag full of bad ingredients.

Merilee sat beside it, putting one paw on it, then looking back at Angelina. "Mrrow?" she asked.

"Fine," Angelina said. "I didn't want to throw out all of that stuff! It's expensive!"

"Mrrow!" Merilee yowled.

"I was going to take it to the magic shop and see if I could return any of it. Get some of my money back. Particularly since that wad of cash that I dropped on Thing Two's coffee table burned up," Angelina complained.

Merilee shook her head. This wasn't going to do. Her sister was backsliding already.

"Mrrow!" Merilee yelled again.

"What? The store isn't open today," Angelina said.

Merilee just glared at her, then walked back into the house.

Angelina followed. "Look, I'll take care of it."

Merilee nodded. Oh yes. Angelina was going to take care of it.

Sooner rather than later.

CHAPTER 28

Merilee yowled.

She hissed.

She howled.

She meowed.

She complained constantly for what seemed like forever, though she was aware that in terms of a human clock, it was probably less than an hour.

Angelina broke eventually.

"Fine. Fine! I'll get rid of the bag."

Merilee ignored her and yelled again. Until she saw some action and movement on the part of her sister, she wasn't about to let up.

Never try to out-stubborn a cat.

Besides, she had lots of other material in her arsenal. All this complaining was making her stomach roil in an uncomfortable fashion.

It wouldn't be much longer before all that lovely chicken was going to come back up.

All over Angelina's favorite shoes. Then her bed. Then maybe Merilee would have to get creative.

Angelina finally put down her coffee (that was at least slightly more bearable without that disgusting soy in it) and went out the back door.

Merilee followed her, making sure that Angelina actually carried the bag full of the bad spell ingredients to the garbage can, then put it in there.

Angelina slammed the cover back on the garbage can hard. As it was a large, green, plastic bin, it didn't make a fulfilling sound, Merilee was sure of it.

"There," Angelina huffed. "Are you satisfied?"

"Mrrr," Merilee said. She was still pissed off at herself. She hadn't noticed that Angelina hadn't actually thrown away the ingredients before this.

Angelina made her way back into the house. However, she deliberately slammed the door shut before Merilee could follow her.

Hmmph!

Merilee tested the protections around Angelina's house. Nope, they were still too strong for her to get through using a portal.

Oh well. Guess that meant she was going to have lounge in the sunlight in the back yard for a while.

Darn.

Merilee made her way to the fragrant grass, stretching out on her side, letting the sun bake her bones and muscles loose, until she felt as though she was made out of soft clay.

Felt like heaven.

She knew that eventually, Angelina would relent and would come and fetch Merilee.

If she didn't, well, Merilee was always ready to serenade her sister again.

In the meanwhile, she was going to take a well-earned rest.

She had a feeling that she was going to need it. It might be the last one for quite some time.

CHAPTER 29

Merilee woke to being delightfully, purrfully stroked. She smelled her sister and the comfort she provided before she bothered opening her eyes.

"Mrrrrow," she said sleepily.

"Mrrrow to you too," Angelina said. She sighed. "I'm sorry. I shouldn't have snapped at you that way. I know I said I wouldn't backslide, into the darker magic. But I think…I think I've been tempted. More tempted than I realized."

"Mrrow," Merilee said, nodding and understanding. She rolled lazily onto her back, and Angelina carefully ran the tips of her fingers along her belly.

"So. I've been thinking about what we need to do to take care of Richard," Angelina said as Merilee rolled back onto her side.

Merilee butted her head against Angelina's hand so that she'd keep stroking Merilee.

"And I think that the best way to get him to stop is to expose him," Angelina said after a few moments.

"Mrrow?" Merilee asked. Why did she get the feeling that she wasn't going to like this?

"I need to collect evidence of bank fraud," Angelina said. "And tax fraud. And all of that is only in his study. At his home."

"Hrrrumph," Merilee said.

Angelina looked at her in surprise. "I didn't know you could make those sorts of sounds."

Merilee tilted her head to one side. Obviously, her sister hadn't been listening.

"Mrrow?" Merilee asked. *Where?*

"He lives north of the city, close to Frontenac State Park, on the bluffs above the Mississippi River," Angelina said. "It's quite a complex. He even has his own tower." Before Merilee hurt something rolling her eyes, Angelina added quietly, "I was so taken by the view. I thought that if I could buy something like that, someday, I'd have made it. You know?"

Merilee was struck by the wistfulness of her sister's tone. She gave a soft, "Mrrow," then poked Angelina's thigh with one paw while gesturing to the incredibly beautiful garden her sister had with her other.

In Merilee's eyes, Angelina had *already* made it.

"True," Angelina said with a soft laugh. "I guess it does depend on the eye of the beholder." She paused for a moment, looking around. "It is beautiful out here. And I don't spend the weekends out here, not like I did when I first got this place." She turned pensive. "I suppose that's from the dark magic as well, isn't it? That feeling as though what you have is never *enough*."

"Mrrow!" Merilee said, agreeing. While as a human she may have been a tiny bit jealous of her big sister Angelina, as a cat, she was perfectly content with who she was, what she was doing.

As long as it didn't involve dying again.

"I checked the schedule, and there is a symphony playing tonight, in town. Which means that Richard is going to be out for the evening," Angelina said. "Wanna do a little breaking and entering?"

Merilee sat back on her butt, looking up at her sister. She didn't like this plan, though she couldn't quite place her paw on what bothered her about it. On the one paw, it might, *might* take care of their problems.

On the other paw, it sounded to her as though Angelina was taking breaking into a really strong Seer's tower too lightly.

"Mrrow?" Marilee said. *How?*

"I've been there before," Angelina assured Merilee. "While you can get into the tower from the main house, that way is guarded, locked, and spell-protected. But I know of a second entrance. More of an escape hatch. The tower sits above the Mississippi, on the bluffs. There's a cave there. All we have to do is go into the cave, then climb up to the tower. That entrance isn't as well protected."

Merilee looked away from Angelina, then back again. She stared hard at her sister.

Are you sure?

Angelina nodded solemnly. "It'll be fine. I think that threatening to expose him is the best way to get him off both of our backs."

Merilee still wasn't certain that this was a good plan. Dick was still going to be coming after them, unless they were very careful how they set up the blackmail material.

However, she didn't have a better one. She gave a deep sigh before pushing her butt up, stretching in all directions before she looked at Angelina again.

"Mrrow?" she said, possibly a bit impatiently.

"We can't go until later on tonight," Angelina said with a

smile. "Plus, I want to prepare a few spells. Do you want to stay out here? Or come inside now?"

Merilee thought for a moment, then started back down the hill, heading toward the house. While the sunlight was glorious at the moment, eventually it would cool off.

"I'm really going to have to install a cat door or something," Angelina muttered.

Merilee wasn't about to suggest that Angelina could just change some of the protection spells, or weave them around Merilee. Or to talk about the portals that Merilee could make herself.

No, it was going to be much more fun watching Angelina try to do something *handy*.

CHAPTER 30

Merilee still didn't feel prepared. Given how her age had advanced with every death, she wondered if she would ever feel like she was ready for anything.

Except for a nice, long nap. Though she'd slept most of the morning out in the back yard, then through a good chunk of the afternoon on a pillow on the couch, she still slept almost the entire ride out to Frontenac State Park. The seat warmer was delightful, and the motion of the car made her drowsy.

Merilee didn't bother opening her eyes until after they'd entered the state park. The smell was what had alerted her. They'd been out in less-tamed countryside for a while. But the state park had a lot older trees in it than the nearby field breaks.

When Angelina parked the car, she paused for a moment, looking over at Merilee. She reached her hand over, letting Merilee butt against it before she assumed that she could start petting.

"You've aged, haven't you?" Angelina said quietly. "Every time you lose a life. You come back older. I can tell. Your fur is less soft, more scraggly. And you're having more difficulty jumping up on things."

Merilee twitched her tail and didn't say anything. What could she say? Her sister was correct. She was aging with every death. Her life was still worth living, and she could still get out and mix it up. Any rabbits or birds, or even butterflies, should still fear her.

"You're also skinnier," Angelina said, running her fingers along Merilee's ribs. "And you sleep more. You snore, which I didn't know kitties could do."

"Hrrrumph," Merilee said.

"It was a very cute snore," Angelina assured her. She paused for a moment. "It occurs to me, though, that maybe you should sit this one out. You don't have many lives left, do you? Three lives?"

Merilee stood up, with her paws on the console between the front seats, staring hard into Angelina's eyes.

You need me.

"Why?" Angelina said, tilting her head to one side. She honestly looked curious.

Dark side.

"Oh," Angelina said after a moment. She didn't blush, but she did look slightly bashful. "I suppose you're right. What, can you smell the darker magic?"

Merilee nodded. Then she leaned forward and licked one of Angelina's hands.

"And taste it as well, on my skin," Angelina said. "I could never hide it from you, could I?"

"Mrrow," Merilee said emphatically. No, Angelina could not. She might think she was being cute or cunning or what have you. She was merely postponing the inevitable cleanup.

And next time, it would be more difficult. Merilee was certain of it.

"All right. No dark magic for me," Angelina said.

Merilee wondered if her sister had just thrown out half the spells she'd prepared.

They'd manage. Somehow.

"I'm pretty sure finding the cave will be easy. As well as the entrance to the tower. It'll be well hidden from outsiders, but I've always been considered an insider, right?" Angelina said with a smile.

Merilee tilted her head from side to side. Any part of this latest quest that was "easy" just meant "suspicious" as far as she was concerned.

Angelina reached over into the back seat, snagging the backpack she'd rigged up. "Hop in," she said.

The bottom of the backpack contained ingredients that Angelina would need for her spells. The top part of it was now made out of plastic, so that Merilee had a good view that way.

Merilee grumbled under her breath but voluntarily went into the bag. It was the best way for her sister to carry her. Merilee's little cat legs could move incredibly fast for a short distance, then she'd have to pause. She couldn't walk beside Angelina for miles. Particularly not since they'd be going over some rough terrain. In addition, Angelina believed that the entrance to the tower was at the top of a ladder in a rock shaft. Really not an easy thing for kitties to climb.

When Angelina hesitated, Merilee gave a warning growl. She could tell that her sister was tempted, now that Merilee was somewhat enclosed, to leave her sister behind.

Angelina didn't realize just how quickly Merilee would be able to leave the car through a portal. In fact, if Angelina did something stupid like that, Merilee would just follow her, sending portals on ahead of her sister and then appearing before her.

That would get annoying quickly for Angelina.

However, even if Angelina had been having second thoughts, she still picked up the backpack and slung it over her shoulders after she'd stepped out of the car.

Tonight, Angelina wore a tight-fitting durable hiking pants that were also breathable and had great stretch, with a navy-blue hoodie. She did have gloves in the pockets, though she doubted that she'd need them. What was Richard going to do? Complain to the police about his illegal files being stolen?

Merilee didn't bother reminding her sister that Dick had already bought the Rochester police. They were on their own. No cops would help them. It was probably why she'd lost her latest life. The cops had orders to kill everything in the room.

After adjusting the bag, and making sure that Merilee was okay, Angelina walked determinedly out of the park, heading toward the river. Though witches couldn't fly, she had prepared a levitation spell. It had taken almost all of the afternoon and eaten up most of the ingredients she'd had on hand. However, it would be a quick way for them to scan the bluff and find the cave entrance.

Merilee didn't really notice a change. First, Angelina was walking on the ground. Then, she was walking in the air. It was kind of cool. She contained her sigh. As a human, she'd never had enough magic to do this sort of thing. As a cat, it wasn't really in her wheelhouse.

Fortunately, It didn't take Angelina long to locate the entrance to the cave. It was close to the tower, though not in a direct line. It was fairly inaccessible. Without magic, or at least some heavy-duty climbing gear, there was no way for anyone to reach it, as it was halfway down the bluff.

The entrance to the tunnel smelled of dust and dried leaves. There were a few bird droppings at the start, but the birds hadn't ventured in very far. Though roots hung down over the entrance, hiding it further, Angelina could easily stand up in it.

Merilee poked her head out of the backpack and over Angelina's shoulder, looking further into the darkness. Angelina paused for a moment, evoking another of her already prepared spells, for improved eyesight—giving herself "cat eyes" as she called it jokingly.

Merilee knew that her own eyesight was better. Still, they were able to use a very dim lamp and still see everything.

Rocks covered the floor of the tunnel, strewn around like a giant child had scattered her building blocks. Water dripped down the walls, the sound of splashing water loud in the quiet night. Merilee rode comfortably in the backpack, though it was tiring for her to stay on her rear legs, standing up. She would look forward for as long as she could, then she would drop down, rest, and stare out behind them, making sure that they were still alone, before standing up again.

Merilee smelled the magic before Angelina, a greasy smell, like burned donuts in hot oil. She stood quickly and tapped Angelina's head.

"What? What is it?" Angelina said.

For the evening, Angelina had also cast an animal language spell on herself, so that she understood everything that Merilee said.

"Mrrow," Merilee said. *Magic.*

"How do you know?" Angelina asked quietly as she raised up the dim light.

What, did she really think she'd be able to see it?

"Smell," Merilee said.

Angelina sniffed, but it was obvious that she couldn't find the odor. "Is it just in front of us? To one side or the other?"

"Step," Merilee instructed her sister.

Angelina obliged, taking one step forward, followed by a second and a third before Merilee stopped them again.

"Left," Merilee said.

"Oohhh!" Angelina exclaimed quietly.

She reached out her hand and did…something. Merilee wasn't quite sure.

What had appeared to be a dark crevice to the side suddenly opened up into a wide passage.

While the tunnel they stood in was natural, this one was obviously man-made. Possibly made with magic, given how smooth the interior of it was.

Merilee purred with pleasure and rubbed her face along Angelina's for a moment, content with the contact between them. She'd never been that much of a toucher before. And possibly, when she'd been a younger cat, such as the day before, she wouldn't have reached out so often to Angelina.

But now, she felt it in her bones, how much she needed the contact. It went beyond soothing. It was communication at a deep level, though she wasn't sure how, or even if, she could ever explain that to her sister.

They stood there for a moment before Angelina raised her dim lantern and cast a bit of a brighter light with it. "Let's go see where this goes, shall we?" she said.

"Yes!" Merilee said.

Time for the next part of their adventure.

CHAPTER 31

The tunnel gave them no surprises. Merilee didn't trust it. Was there some other magic here, that she wasn't sensing? What if it wasn't magical, but mechanical? An alarm that they'd set off by walking down here?

Still, no one came racing after them. No large flock of carnivorous bats started dive bombing them. Everything seemed rather civilized, actually.

They reached the ladder. It was metal, with short rungs, and shot up straight into the rock shaft above them. Angelina shone her light upward, but the darkness stubbornly repelled it.

"I don't like it," Angelina said softly.

"Agreed," Merilee meowed. She looked up, considering the amount of space between each rung.

"Hey, what are you doing?" Angelina said as Merilee stepped on her sister's head, pulling herself out of the backpack.

Without further comment, Merilee launched herself from her sister's shoulder, onto the ladder.

"What, are you going to climb up that yourself?" Angelina asked, bemused.

It was going to take her some time, sure. But Merilee made a *much* smaller target.

Whatever was up there, waiting to get them, was going to be expecting something human sized.

"Catch me if I fall," Merilee instructed Angelina as she carefully balanced, then pulled herself up the next rung.

Her shoulder muscles were going to be *so sore* the next day. So were her butt muscles. Hell, all her muscles.

But Merilee kept climbing the ladder, one rung at a time.

The darkness seemed endless. She could barely see the light at the bottom, where Angelina stood. Up above, there was just inky black.

Again, Merilee smelled the magic before it struck her. She pulled back just in time as a sharp blade whirled from one side of the shaft to the other, sliding easily through the opening between two rungs.

Merilee went up even more slowly now, raising a paw between rungs.

There were two more circular saw blades, a sword, six darts, and a heavy stone that dropped from above. Angelina swore after that one fell, but it appeared to have missed her.

Finally, Merilee was at the top. Automatic lights came on, probably connected to a motion detector. She yowled down the tunnel, "Come up!"

Then she looked guiltily around her. Hopefully no one had heard that.

The platform she stood on appeared to be a staging area. Round, like the shaft that had held the ladder, carved out of the same rock, just several feet bigger. Empty metal shelves lined one area, while what smelled to be a black bug-out bag sat just before a beige metal door leading somewhere. The shelves, the floor, and even the air were dusty, as if someone's cleaning spells weren't up to par.

It wasn't until Merilee approached the door that she sensed the magic embedded there. It had been set deep into the rock surrounding the door itself. Attacking the door wouldn't get you anywhere.

She paused, considering. What would it take to get through the door? The walls? Did Angelina have the magic necessary?

"Thanks for the warning about the falling rock," Angelina said sarcastically as she crested the tunnel.

There had only been so much Merilee could do. She had gotten the pair of them past all the traps, hadn't she?

"I figured this way would be easier," Angelina said, nodding with approval after looking around some. "Magic's in the walls, right? Not the door?"

"Yes," Merilee said. She sat back, curious what Angelina would do next.

Angelina set her backpack down on the floor and started pulling out ingredients. Using pink chalk, Angelina quickly drew a small circle on the floor, just in front of the door. She scrawled some runes in it. Interestingly, the lines in them were straighter. They weren't the squiggly ones she'd been using earlier. Then Angelina pulled out a mirror and placed it in the center.

Huh. That was different. She wasn't trying to break through. She was merely trying to see what was on the other side. Physical attacks were expected. Some spell attacks probably were as well.

But a little spying? That might slip under the radar.

It only took Angelina a few moments to connect her mirror with something that stood on the other side of the wall. Shadowy bands kept running across the image.

Wait. Had Angelina connected to a computer monitor on the other side? One running a screen saver program?

That was a good use for a mirror-spying spell. Merilee was impressed.

It appeared to be a plain study on the other side of the door. There was more than one computer monitor on the desk. They appeared to be staring out of the center of three, all of them showing endless loops of dancing light beams for the screen saver.

Next to the desk stood tall cabinets. Even in the dark, Merilee could see the glow of the protective sigils around them. Beside that was a chaise lounge with a lamp over it, perfect for reading or napping. Another door stood opposite the computer, probably leading into the rest of the tower. Even more shelves graced the walls, filled with books and ingredients that Merilee knew she'd never have been able to afford.

The good news was that there wasn't anyone in the room. The door leading out to the rest of the tower was probably locked and spelled.

The bad news was that they were still on *this* side of the wall, not in the actual tower itself.

How were they going to get in?

"There are too many spells for a portal to get through," Angelina murmured. "And after we get inside, well, there are still going to be so many spells to unlock."

Merilee stared at the door. Her attention kept getting caught not by the lock, or the handle, where Angelina was focusing, but by the other side, where the hinges were visible.

Hinges.

Sure, the door was locked. The walls had protection spells in them.

What about the hinges?

She walked around the circle, getting closer to the door.

Plain metal. No real protection.

How much magic would it take to pry one of those up?

Only about as much as what it took to open the refrigerator, Merilee discovered.

"Over here!" she squawked excitedly.

Angelina finally walked over to see what Merilee was up to.

She looked at the pin on the ground under the bottom hinge, then back to the door.

"Really?" she asked. "That's all it's going to take?"

Merilee shrugged. Smart guys like Dick were going to be all about the magical protections, or the door locks.

No one ever looked at the construction of the door, how it was actually held in place in the doorframe.

Angelina easily popped the two other hinge bolts. The door stayed exactly where it was, but both of them felt the easing of the magical spells.

The spells worked in a circle, like the tower. They had been weakened by the door no longer being fully attached.

It didn't take much for Angelina to disarm the few spells that remained across the door, then sliding the door out of the jamb.

"Huh," Angelina said as she pushed it to the side. "I never would have thought of that. Thank you."

Merilee purred and butted her head against Angelina's calf.

She didn't say, "I told you so," but hopefully Angelina heard it anyway.

Angelina needed Merilee, just as Merilee needed her big sister.

That was the way the world worked.

CHAPTER 32

Angelina packed away all her spell ingredients into the backpack, insisting that Merilee climb back in too, before they entered Dick the Elf's study.

All the hair raised up on the hackles of Merilee's back as they crossed the threshold. It felt like trying to crawl out from under wool blankets in the middle of winter, the static electricity sparking.

"Hurry," Merilee told Angelina. No physical alarm had just been raised—she didn't hear warning klaxons ringing in the distance. She'd still felt *something* passing through the solid rock wall of the tower.

Something that was meant as a warning.

Angelina nodded and walked right over to the cabinet. The hinges on it were unfortunately hidden. As soon as Angelina called up her first spell, a huge glowing circle of protection formed across the center of the cabinet. Glowing red letters squiggled across it. It stank of dried blood and rotting wood.

Great.

Angelina worked at the protection spells, trying to tug

them apart, while Merilee kept watch, looking out the back of the backpack.

It wasn't difficult to see the door to the room opening slowly, even in the dim glow of just the computer screen and the protection circle.

However, it took Merilee a few moments to figure out what she was looking at.

It wasn't a human, for all that it waddled on its back feet. It wasn't wearing a gray shirt and pants, despite its color— no, that gray was the color of its fur. Nor did it have on a mask. Its natural coloring gave it that look, with a black band across its eyes. It had a rancid odor, as though its last meal had been left to rot in the sun for a week, to tenderize it.

Was this Dick's familiar? A raccoon? Or was this just hired muscle, because he knew he might be facing a mighty pissed-off cat?

With an ear-splitting yowl, Merilee launched herself from Angelina's back. The force of her jump knocked her sister forward, almost onto those deadly runes.

Merilee couldn't issue an apology, though. She was too busy hissing and distracting the newcomer.

She just had to give Angelina time to get through the protection spells on the cupboard. Then they could grab what they needed to get Dick off their backs.

This interloper had a greater reach than Merilee. And its black claws were devilishly sharp. It chittered madly at her, not making any sense. Its eyes reflected the red glow of the protection runes.

Crap. Was that foam she was seeing around its muzzle?

Only *Dick the Elf* would have a rabid raccoon as a familiar. Its name was probably Rocky.

Merilee swatted at the raccoon. She didn't care that much if she hit it or not. She needed to judge its reflexes.

Pretty dang fast, it turned out, as she backed up abruptly, neatly missing being blinded.

Merilee growled at the thing and backed up slowly.

Just come this way, you disgusting thing…

It appeared to work, at least for a while. The rabid raccoon was totally focused on Merilee, forgetting the bigger danger, which was Angelina working diligently in the corner.

Though the room was round. It was a tower, after all. Did towers really have corners?

Merilee shook her head. She needed to focus!

How could she get rid of this damned beast?

The rabid raccoon advanced on Merilee slowly. It grinned madly.

Ugh. Was that a piece of fur stuck to its teeth?

Merilee felt her back pressing up against the legs of the desk. Where could she go now?

Without a thought, she jumped up onto the desk. There wasn't much room there. She knocked things down, onto the raccoon's head. Pencil holder. Mouse. Mousepad. The keyboard was connected, otherwise she would have dumped that as well.

The raccoon suddenly jumped up onto the desk and raced toward her. Crap!

Merilee hissed and slashed out with her claws, getting in a good swipe along the creature's jowl line. Just a little lower and she might have hit something vital. Or higher, and blinded the thing.

But that might have put her paw too close to its jaws, which snapped at her.

His black paws picked up the keyboard and swung it at her. That gave him a greater reach than just his claws.

The edge of the keyboard connected solidly with Merilee's shoulder. She yowled her dismay. That *hurt*.

All of Merilee's fur was standing on end now. Her tail was all poofed out.

Unless she had a magical way of increasing her size and strength, she was outweighed. Raccoons were predators of all housecats who'd gone feral.

She raced forward and slashed at the creature again. He held the keyboard up like a shield, protecting his face from her slash.

Which left the lower part of his belly exposed. She sliced across his fur nicely, and six long beaded trails of blood showed up there.

Good.

However, she didn't back up quickly enough, and he brought the keyboard smashing down on her paw.

Merilee howled loud enough to wake the dead.

Damn it! That alerted someone. An alarm rang somewhere in the distance.

Crap. The stupid raccoon turned his attention from her and looked toward Angelina.

Merilee couldn't afford to split her attention.

She did notice something she hadn't seen before. Directly behind the monitor they'd been looking out of stood a window.

A window that was already cracked open slightly, letting in the cool night air. A screen was all that stood between her and the outside.

Merilee slashed at the raccoon again, this time catching it in the face. She tore his ear, as well as the corner of his eye.

But the raccoon caught her paw before she could withdraw, biting down hard.

Merilee couldn't help but scream again. Particularly as she felt the poison from the damned thing entering her bloodstream.

Damn it! Regular rabies didn't work that fast. But this was magically enhanced.

She was going to die from the poison before Angelina could get her to a healer. She knew that much.

Might as well take the stupid beast down with her.

Merilee bunched herself up, wriggling her butt once to make sure that she was stable.

Then she *launched* herself at the raccoon, carrying them both over the monitor (knocking it over in the process) and smashing against the open window.

The screen had protection spells on it. Of course.

However, those spells were only to keep things from the *outside* getting in. Nothing was there to prevent her from shoving her way out, from slicing through the screen from the *inside*.

The raccoon was too stupid to realize what was going on. He tussled with her, his jaws clamped firmly on her neck, intent on killing her.

Not realizing that they were falling several stories down from a tower window.

The pain of the damned raccoon's teeth seared into Merilee's bones. It was worse than anything she'd experienced before. She did her best with her claws and her own teeth, tearing at the stupid thing, all the while keeping them angled correctly, so that *he* would land first.

Just before they reached the ground the raccoon appeared to recognize his danger. He scrambled for a moment but it was too late.

He hit the ground with a satisfying *crack*, his spine breaking.

Just before Merilee's legs and neck broke as well, sending her into blissful darkness.

～

Merilee woke standing on the bluff, overlooking the Mississippi River. It was peaceful here. Kind of pretty. It wouldn't be a bad spot to spend all of eternity. Plus, she was pretty sure she could annoy the hell out of Dick the Elf. Figure out some way to make noise while she was haunting him.

However, Angelina still needed her. And while annoying Dick would be nice, stopping him would be even better.

Still, Merilee stayed where she was for a while, watching all the color drain out of the world, the soft yellow of the bluffs, the pretty greens of the wild grasses and the trees, the pale blue-black of the sky. Before everything grew gray and ghostly, she made her way over to the portal.

This time was better, at least in some ways. Sure, her paws still felt as though they were on fire. Her back hurt, and every step was made with a broken spine. But the surrounding air was gentler. Her soul didn't hurt as much. It wasn't as much of a drag going through to the other side.

Once she reached the ground again, Merilee paused, giving the restful circle of light off to the side a good, long look.

It was in paw-reach. It wouldn't be difficult at all to step over into it, to stop this endless circle of life and death.

As always, it was thoughts of her sister that drove her away, back into the darkness. Angelina needed her, or else Dick was going to win.

Merilee turned her back on the peace and tranquility she knew awaited for her, and instead, plunged back into the darkness and life.

LIFE EIGHT

CHAPTER 33

Merilee came back to life sitting peacefully on the bluff, overlooking the Mississippi River. She wore her white fur. It was still night, but she could smell the dawn in the air. Birds had yet to rise. The river moved quickly through its channel, a soft slushing sound. Everything seemed hopeful and new.

Then a shiver went through her, as if the last of the other plane that she'd come through had now passed fully from her and she was back in the real world. Her joints ached. As did her teeth. She was cold, and would soon be shivering, at least until the sun came out and baked her. Probably getting too hot in the process.

Where was Angelina? Was she still in the tower? Had she already left? Driven away? Or was she searching for Merilee?

Merilee closed her eyes, lifted her nose, and sniffed the air, trying to tease apart all the scents she smelled.

No, Angelina wasn't anywhere close by.

Merilee turned and looked at the tower. Though she couldn't say for certain, she'd bet that Angelina was no longer there, either.

After turning a few tight circles, Merilee created her first portal back to the car. She knew the general direction she was going, and trusted her magical senses to get her there.

However, every portal she created (and it took three) drained her. She was practically dragging herself across the pavement after the last one, heading directly toward Angelina's white Lexus.

There were no protection spells on the car itself. It would only take one more portal for Merilee to project herself inside.

She paused, collecting herself, gathering up what little strength she had remaining.

Suddenly, hands scooped her up from behind.

Merilee hissed and yowled, twisting, her claws out and ready to scratch.

She stopped herself just before she slashed across Angelina's face.

"There you are!" Angelina said, hugging Merilee too tightly to her chest. "I've been looking for you for hours."

Merilee could smell both the tears that Angelina had cried, as well as the frustration in her sweat. "Mrrow," she said softly, nuzzling into Angelina's neck as her sister loosened her grip, content to just be held for a few moments.

"Where were you? Are you all right? You're so skinny," Angelina complained. "And light. You weigh less than you did." Tears came again. "I'm sorry, I'm so, so sorry."

"Mrrow?" Merilee asked.

"I didn't get anything we could use. I couldn't break through the protection spells fast enough to open the cupboard before someone came. I had to flee." She sighed.

Merilee nodded, rubbing her head up and down along Angelina's chin. It was all right. It hadn't been the best plan in the world to start with.

They'd just have to come up with something different.

After a good, long nap.

"Mrrow?"

"Yes, home for now," Angelina said. She opened the car and carefully placed Merilee on the seat before hurrying over to the driver side.

Merilee rolled her eyes when Angelina cast a worried look at her as she started the car. Sure, she wasn't in the best shape. But she wasn't about to fall apart.

Then the heat on the seat warmer started. Merilee started to purr.

"I can hear you over the engine, now," Angelina said with a smile. "You've got quite a rumble going."

Merilee nodded and closed her eyes. That was only how it should be.

Angelina would discover soon enough that just as Merilee's purr had gotten louder, her determination had gotten stronger as well.

They were going to have to take Dick the Elf out once and for all.

Merilee woke when they reached Angelina's house. She insisted on getting out of the car herself. She tried to hide the little exclamation of pain and annoyance as she jumped down.

Damn it. Her hips really were going.

Once inside, they ate quickly, Angelina making both of them eggs, hers fried, Merilee's raw, with some of the cooked chicken breast mixed in.

Angelina didn't even complain when Merilee insisted on her bowl being put on the kitchen table, so that they could eat together.

"You need protein," Angelina said as Merilee finished licking her bowl clean. "Anything else?"

Merilee considered for a moment, pausing as she washed her face. She could use some more water, and possibly something for the pain in her hips, but other than that, no, she didn't need more.

"Mrrow," Merilee said as kind of a placeholder. Was it time for a nap? She glanced at Angelina, who was looking thoughtfully at her.

"How did you get to the car on your own?" Angelina asked as she sipped her coffee. Luckily, the bad magic appeared to be wearing off, as she'd taken one good whiff of the chemicals in those icky syrups of hers and had refrained, instead reaching reluctantly for actual, real sugar.

Though Merilee was still tired, she figured now was as good a time as any to show Angelina.

She hopped off the table (still with that small yelp) and walked to the middle of the kitchen floor. Then she paced in a tight circle, once, twice, three times.

A small portal popped up on the floor.

"Wait, what?" Angelina said, rising. "You can just transport yourself places?" She sounded angry.

"Mrrow?" Merilee said, looking up at her sister patiently. Hadn't she said that she was far stronger magically as a cat than she'd been as a human?

"Wow," Angelina said, rocking back on her heels as she considered the implications. "That's how cats just appear places, isn't it? Like between your legs when you aren't looking?"

Merilee just waited.

"Can you make a bigger one? For me?" Angelina asked.

Merilee considered the size of the portal in front of her. Before, when she'd been younger, maybe she could have. Maybe. Right now, though…

"Mrrow," she said sorrowfully. A larger portal just wasn't possible.

"That's all right," Angelina said. She crouched down so she could run her fingers along Merilee's jowl, bringing out loud purrs. "It's good to know, though, that you can always get to someplace on your own." She paused, then said, "If I change the protection spells on the house, you wouldn't need a cat door, would you?"

Merilee twitched her tail in a feline shrug. She wasn't about to admit to that. Then she gave a face-splitting yawn.

She'd been awake far too long that morning. It was the perfect time for that first post-breakfast nap.

"Fine," Angelina said, laughing as she stood. "I have some things to get ready. Then we're going to have to talk about how to go after Richard."

At Merilee's eyeroll, she said, "Fine. Dick. Dick the Elf," she added with a grin.

Good. Merilee nodded with approval.

Richard Keebler was a big, important man. Someone who even the Mighty Angelina had looked up to. Been awed by. Possibly even slightly intimidated by.

Dick the Elf was someone they could fight. Beat. And win.

Merilee sauntered off to her pillow on the couch for a well-deserved nap.

CHAPTER 34

Try as they might, neither Merilee or Angelina could come up with a satisfying plan for dealing with Dick the Elf that day. It was a Sunday, something Merilee tried to wrap her head around. She'd been chased from her house by the three thugs Tuesday night, transforming herself into a cat. It hadn't even been a week. Yet she'd already lost most of her lives.

There was a nagging sense that possibly she was meant to die that first night, that she should have been killed on Tuesday. All these lives were just borrowed time.

She didn't bother trying to convey that to Angelina. She didn't want to worry her sister.

Particularly since Angelina appeared to be worried enough already. Merilee kept catching the looks that Angelina gave her, concerned looks about the state of Merilee's health.

All right, so maybe she'd lost a couple of teeth eating breakfast that morning. And possibly a few of her claws were so split she'd end up hurting herself rather than hurting someone else if she tried slicing them apart.

And her fur…yeah. Okay. Her fur was no longer anywhere near as luxurious as it had once been.

Still, she didn't have any regrets. She just had to make sure that she went out with a bang.

A big enough one to take Dick with her.

"You know that I'm going to have to go to work tomorrow, right?" Angelina said that night as she made dinner. Though Merilee no longer could appreciate a fine marinara sauce over pasta, she still thought it smelled good.

Nothing artificial. Angelina had thrown out a bunch of chemicals from her pantry, sighing at the expense. She explained to Merilee that she'd at one point been a pretty good cook without all those fancy things. She could get back to that.

"Mrrow," Merilee said, disapproving. Surely Angelina had enough sick time saved up that she could afford to take a couple more days off?

"Just for a few hours in the morning," Angelina assured her. "I won't be long."

"Mrrow," Merilee said firmly. *No.*

Angelina sighed. "I know. I know. But Sue has some questions for me. And I really need to go in."

Merilee jumped up onto the counter and walked cautiously toward the stove. She knew that the sauce Angelina had put together could bubble and spatter, and she *really* didn't want to have to clean that sauce off her nice white fur.

Especially since she'd spent so long this afternoon getting it to lie right, hiding the few patches of skin that now showed.

"Mrrow," Merilee said again, demanding Angelina's full attention.

Angelina turned the burner down and caught Merilee's

eye, long enough so that Merilee could get the concept across.

Not alone.

"I can't take you into the office," Angelina said. "There's a strict 'no pet' policy. If there weren't, we'd be dealing with Jim's hunting dogs. Believe me, you don't want one of those things slobbering on you on a regular basis."

Merilee thought for a moment, then she *Mrrow*ed again, keeping Angelina's attention on her.

She carefully made her way across the countertop, heading for the far corner, where Angelina kept her breadbox. (And the stuff in there was *definitely* going to have to go as well. It was made from a few ingredients held together with a mass of chemicals. Yuck.)

Though the kitchen was fairly well lit, this corner held some shadows. After making sure that Angelina was still watching, Merilee growled loud in her chest, paced back and forth a couple of times before stepping into the shadow.

The look of astonishment on Angelina's face was worth every ounce of energy that it had taken to get the damned shadows to cooperate.

"You can just hide? Like that? Even in a well-lit place like this?" Angelina demanded, sounding both pissed off as well as a little envious.

Merilee stepped back out again into the light. She cocked her head to the side, waiting for Angelina to see the implications of such a thing.

"So if I take you to the office, you can just hide in one of the conference rooms, right? No one will be able to see you," Angelina said, musing.

"Mrrow," Merilee said. She'd be hiding under Angelina's

desk, not off in some conference room. But on the whole, Angelina had it right.

"Fine, you can come with me," Angelina said. Then she gave Merilee a grin. "And you'll make sure I don't stay too long as well, right?"

"Mrrow," Merilee said firmly. *Affirmative.*

Though Merilee had never been that close to her sister while they'd been growing up—there had been too much rivalry between them—she was glad that they had the opportunity to get to know each other better now.

She'd never realized that Angelina was such a messy eater. Must be the "dog person" inside of her.

Despite being told how "unhealthy" meat was, Angelina still served herself good portions of it on a regular basis. She explained that it just meant that she ate a lot of salads when she was with other people.

Hopefully, Merilee could break her of her habit and continual need to compare herself to others.

Merilee certainly no longer needed to. She was a magnificent cat. Who could come close to her brilliance?

The pair of them spent the night cuddled up together on the sofa, Angelina splitting her time between consulting old spell books and watching a silly rom-com movie, while Merilee curled up next to her, pressing her back against the warmth of her sister's thigh, purring and sleeping.

The next morning, though Merilee woke up with the birds, she didn't bother doing more than getting up, stretching, drinking a little water, then going back to sleep until Angelina got up.

Then, it was a race. Outside to do her business. Inside to eat. Angelina gathered up everything, forgetting her glasses the first time, then one of her spell books the second time before they got out to the car.

Merilee jumped more easily onto the passenger seat this time. Hmmm. Maybe she was getting used to this age.

Or maybe she'd finally slept enough and felt renewed.

She suspected the feeling wouldn't last, as the warmth of the seat lulled her back into a quick nap.

Angelina parked in her usual spot. Merilee climbed over to the driver's side then out the open door.

"Mrrow?" she said, rubbing her side along Angelina's shin.

"I'll be fine," Angelina said after a bit. "Funny. I used to love my work. Used to thrive on the competition and the power games. Now, it kind of seems silly, you know?"

"Mrrow," Merilee said, agreeing. It was why she had such a low paying, low prestige job. She'd never cared for the rat race, as it were.

"You want me to get you into the building?" Angelina said. She held up the backpack.

"Mrrow," Merilee said. She'd say *please* if she could. Hopefully Angelina heard it anyway.

Angelina had modified the backpack again so that Merilee could no longer see out the back of it. Which meant that Angelina was no longer as safe. Merilee couldn't protect her sister as well as she'd like. It also meant that no one could see Angelina smuggle Merilee in.

"This feels so much more comfortable, carrying books this way," Angelina said quietly. "Why did I think I needed a briefcase? Particularly one that always made me feel as if I were going to lose my arm carrying it?"

Merilee knew. It was part of Angelina's bid to fit in.

She didn't bother pointing out that Angelina's outfit that morning was much more sensible than what she normally wore to the office. Her soft, off-white blouse actually fit her, instead of being too tight. Her skirt was looser as well as longer, made out of navy-blue cotton.

Angelina still wore kitten heels, which was only appropriate.

Merilee didn't like being in such an enclosed, dark space. It gave her bad flashbacks to being stuck in a burlap bag, the one that the thugs had used to drown her.

Still, she settled down as best she could. She spent her time ferreting out all the different scents. First, there was the parking garage, that stank of oil and gas, along with exhaust. Then they were outside for a bit. She could hear the birds in the park across the street, the cars driving too fast down the quiet road. The wind carried that all-too-present scent of humans, along with a faint whiff of coffee from an outdoor cart they passed.

Then it was up the stairs, into the building. Inside, she heard the sound of many human feet crossing the broad marble floors, talking softly to each other, no one wanting to break the quiet of the morning. The cleaner used on the floors carried the smell of fake lemon, but as she didn't catch any hint of dust underneath it, it was probably effective.

Up a quick elevator ride (and wow, did that feel different to Merilee, both as a cat and because she was riding in a bag), then into the office.

As they crossed the threshold, Merilee felt a quick pass of some sort of magic.

Who else was magical in the office? Why was the door protected? What was it supposedly protecting the people inside from?

She didn't like it. She didn't have space in the pack to start grooming herself, but she really wanted to straighten out the fur that had been mussed up by that spell.

Angelina paused, and Merilee heard Sue's voice, asking them about their weekend, if the mysterious cat had been cleared up.

"Oh, yes," Angelina said. "Turned out it had belonged to

my sister Merilee. She'd gotten into a bit of a fix," she confided. "I got her out."

"Good for you!" Sue enthused.

Merilee wasn't certain, but she thought the woman was lying. If only she could see! She'd gotten really good at spotting Angelina's lies.

"So everything's taken care of?" Sue asked. She sounded slightly disappointed, as if she'd wanted to take part of the adventure.

"No, not really," Angelina admitted. "I'm only here for the morning. I'm going to have to take the afternoon off."

"But what about the Fredrickson case?" Sue said, practically whining.

Merilee braced herself for the disappointment of her sister forgetting her promises to Merilee, that she'd only be here in the office for a short while, that then they'd spend the afternoon figuring out what to do about Dick.

"I can't continue with it," Angelina said firmly. Possibly even a little coolly. "You're going to have to get Marti to take it, or someone else."

Hmmm. What exactly did that mean? Merilee wasn't certain.

Had Angelina actually come to see the light? To understand that this wasn't a good place? Merilee couldn't actually smell the greed and corruption, but she knew it was there, just under the surface.

Angelina had joked more than once that she worked for the only honest law firm in town.

Merilee wondered now if that was true.

Angelina had her own office, a small but quiet space. Merilee instantly felt better in there, her fur settling down.

However, Angelina didn't close the door. She'd already explained that she couldn't. That would have been a sign that something was wrong. If she had a private phone call she could. Otherwise, the door had to be open. Merilee just had to hide.

Angelina put her backpack on the floor, opening it up.

Merilee didn't say anything but jumped out before Angelina started pulling files and books out.

"You know, I hate to say this, but I think there's something wrong with Sue," Angelina said softly. "I'd never thought about it before. She was the one who introduced me to Dick."

Merilee bobbed her head up and down for a brief moment, giggling that she'd finally gotten Angelina to stop calling him Richard.

"You be careful around her," Angelina warned. Then she sighed.

Merilee rated it low on the kitty scale. Perhaps a 4.2. If she was being generous.

"I really do have some work to do this morning. Particularly since I'm taking the rest of the day off," Angelina said. "Will you be okay down there?"

"Mrrow," Merilee said softly.

She curled up in a dark corner, hidden in the shadows. No one would be able to see her. Even Angelina had to squint to catch a glimpse of her.

"Thanks," Angelina said as she went to work.

Merilee was worried about her sister. Worried about the pair of them being in this office.

It felt like a trap.

Hopefully, no one realized that Merilee was there too, that the surprise she'd bring would offset the mistake they'd made by coming here.

CHAPTER 35

It didn't surprise Merilee in the least when she woke up to the sound of Sue's voice.

"There's a client in the Heights conference room," Sue said. "Can you do the intake on him? Carol is also out this morning, and everyone else is too swamped."

"Sure," Angelina said, as though she didn't mind.

Merilee knew that she minded. Quite a bit.

Angelina was a paralegal. She really shouldn't have to do a secretary's job. Merilee had heard her complain about it plenty of times before.

Still, Angelina gathered up her notebook and followed Sue out.

Strange. Just after Angelina had left, Sue closed the door of Angelina's office. Firmly.

As if she was trying to keep some ordinary cat from escaping.

Merilee rolled her eyes. Sue might know a little about magic (and come to think of it, how did she know? Merilee had forgotten to ask Angelina about her). However, Sue knew *nothing* about Merilee.

Now, where was Angelina?

Merilee raised her nose to the air. The false scents of Angelina were still threaded through the air. It honestly made the real smell of her easier to track.

Not too far away.

Wait, was that fear that Merilee caught in Angelina's scent?

As quickly as she could, Merilee formed a portal, stepping through from the office into the corner of a conference room.

Angelina sat at one end of a small conference table, her notebook forgotten.

A well-dressed man sat at the other end of the table. He reminded Merilee of a younger William H. Macy, clean cut, clean shaven, though he was more of a ginger than the actor, with the same wide forehead, big ears, and piercing blue eyes. He had a boyish grin that showed off his dimples.

He smelled of rotten peaches and styrofoam, plastic gunk woven between putrid stalks of garlic.

Merilee instantly knew who she was dealing with. *Dick the Elf* needed no introduction.

How could Angelina have ever thought this was a *good* man?

"It's so nice of your sister to join us," he said smoothly, looking directly at Merilee though she'd hidden herself neatly in the corner.

Could he actually see her? How accurately? Merilee narrowed her eyes at him, then sauntered off to the other corner.

Dick kept looking expectantly in the corner where she'd first arrived.

Hmmmm.

With a delicate leap, Merilee hopped up onto the conference table.

Dick started, then narrowed his eyes at her. "I thought you'd moved. Good to know I shouldn't underestimate you, that I need to trust my senses."

Merilee merely sniffed at him, sat her butt down, then started licking one of her front paws, using it to wash her face, completely nonchalantly.

"Being trapped like that, as a cat, must be painful," he said.

What, was he trying to sympathize with her?

"My mama, bless her heart, always told me that you could catch more flies with honey than with vinegar," he said.

Merilee rolled her eyes. Did he really think that this innocent, plain-talking, good ol' boy routine was working on her?

She glanced hurriedly at Angelina, then breathed a sigh of relief.

Good. It wasn't working on her sister, either.

Angelina looked pissed, as well as slightly disgusted.

They'd have to work on her forgiving herself later, for how Dick had tricked her. For now, the pair of them needed to stay focused on what was directly in front of them.

Namely, this dick.

"So I brought you something," Dick said. "I'm going to reach inside my pocket and take out an amulet," he added, actions slowly matching his words.

Huh. Was he afraid of Angelina? Merilee remembered that Dick was actually more of a Seer than a witch. He predicted natural disasters.

And Angelina, when she got really pissed off, could call down a thunderstorm.

Maybe even a tornado?

Interesting thought.

The amulet that Dick slid across the table didn't smell wrong. Not like he did, and the rest of his magic.

No, it smelled rich, like fresh cream, with a delicious roast beef scent underneath, and Merilee didn't even like her food cooked anymore.

It was the size of a silver dollar, made out of wood, with hard-lined runes carved into it, not the squiggly shapes that Merilee associated with the darker magics.

"Go on, take it," Dick said. "It isn't a trap. It's that honey I was mentioning earlier."

Merilee sniffed it, then batted it over to Angelina with her paw. It skittered across the smooth table quickly, landing in front of her sister.

"What is it?" Angelina said.

"You tell me," Dick said, sounding like a patient tutor.

"It's some sort of transformation spell," Angelina said. "As well as something about origins."

"Exactly!" Dick said, proud and pleased. "See, I knew you had it in you, kiddo."

Merilee didn't bother containing her hiss in response to that.

Dick wasn't a parental figure. He wasn't a *friend* or a teacher. He was the enemy.

Merilee would always remember that, even if Angelina might forget.

"What does it do?" Angelina asked.

"It can help Merilee return to her human form," Dick said quietly. "Without kicking off the 'lost life' clause that generally occurs when a witch transforms into a cat and starts losing lives."

"Mrrow?" Merilee said, curious.

"You aren't the only witch who's thought that she could get away with losing cat lives instead of her human life,"

Dick lectured. "Many have tried before you. It almost always ends badly."

"Hrrrmph," Merilee said. She hadn't transformed into a cat in order to "get away" with something. She'd been trying to escape from his thugs.

His now dead thugs.

She looked at Angelina, who was still studying the coin.

"So this is the honey," she said slowly. "What do you want in return for it?"

"Why, you, of course!" Dick said with that wide, *aw shucks* smile of his.

Merilee already hated it.

"I just need you to work through the end of the quarter. Then, if you truly want to leave, we can part amicably," Dick said.

Did he really believe that Angelina was going to fall for that? If Angelina went back, she'd lose her soul.

Or worse, would end up selling it to him.

"I don't want to work for you anymore," Angelina said primly. "I never should have followed your lead in the first place, working with the darker magic. That was a mistake on my part."

"What, you should have stayed a good witch? Following along beside Miss Goody Two-Shoes, over here? Or maybe I should call her Four Shoes?" Dick asked, grinning at his own wit.

Angelina lifted her chin defiantly. "That's my sister," she said coolly.

"That's your *loser* sister," Dick clarified. "Your words. Not mine."

Merilee shrugged. She'd said a few choice words about the Almighty Angelina in the before times as well.

Didn't mean anything now.

"You don't have as much power as a good witch, following all the rules," Dick said. "You can't do as much. Can't affect as much. You can do good following the darker magics, you know."

Angelina shook her head. "Can't do enough good to counter the harm you cause," she said.

"What harm?" Dick said. "I'm making money from the stock market. Easy money that I'm willing to share with you. I don't give a damn how many orphans or puppies you save with your take. You just need to continue giving me mine."

Merilee tilted her head to the side, curious. For all his "good ol' boy" act, Dick sure was impatient. And not very nice.

"And when do you have enough?" Angelina asked. "Can you define what would constitute that?"

"What do you mean?" Dick asked, obviously perplexed by the entire concept.

"When will you have enough money? Enough fame? Enough power?" Angelina sneered. "I don't think there's ever enough for your kind. No, you want to sit in the middle of your spiderweb forever, sucking the life out of whatever and whoever you touch, dropping their husks and reaching for the next one. There's never going to be enough. I could work for you this quarter, but then something else would come up. And it would be the next quarter. And the next year. Until I'm all used up as well, and you move on to the next victim."

Merilee preened with pride at the tone her sister was taking.

"And is that your final word?" Dick said.

He was trying for friendly. Even casual. But the sound of an ominous threat was woven through all of his words.

"It is," Angelina said, sitting back, waiting.

"Well, then I'm sorry to do this, but you leave me no choice, young lady," Dick said.

He waved one hand in the air negligibly.

The magical circle that had been drawn on the entire table suddenly lit up with a deadly red glow.

And Merilee was in the center of it.

Abruptly, she couldn't breathe. Her fur had caught on fire. The smoke blinded her, choked her. She found herself coughing, unable to take a deep breath and clear her throat.

She couldn't move. Her muscles were caught firmly, and she had to sit still as she was burning up. If only she could pace! Maybe she could create a portal. Something. Anything to end the agony.

She couldn't even howl her displeasure. Damn Dick! Damn him and all of his ilk, who believed they were better than everyone else and who always had to have their way.

If she could, Merilee would scratch his eyes out. Bite down hard on his jugular, spilling out his life's blood. She would bet it tasted rotten.

Damn it! Why was this death taking so long? She was in an agony of burning, being taken apart by inches. Death by a thousand flames.

It took a lot of concentration to see beyond the smoke.

Angelina was being physically restrained by Dick. Obviously, her sister was trying to reach her. Reach for her. Help her, someway.

Merilee forced herself to look down. She was engulfed in blue flame. Which might be pretty if it didn't *hurt so damned much*.

She kept circling back to the pain. It was stealing her life, inch by inch.

The crackling (cackling?) of the fire blocked her ears. She couldn't hear what Angelina and Dick were saying.

What that bastard was getting Angelina to agree to.

What Angelina had said before was true though. No matter what sort of time limit she put on her services, Dick would find a way to prolong it.

Angelina was starting to break down. To agree to whatever the hell Dick was proposing.

Merilee wasn't having any of it.

It took a supreme amount of effort, but slowly she lifted on wicked claw up off the table.

Damn it! This was taking too long.

She fought herself. Fought the agony. Fought to remain conscious through it all, to not give in.

Angelina didn't understand the nature of the spell that encased Merilee.

Merilee did.

As long as she was whole, she'd keep burning. Forever, if Dick had his say. All her nerves on fire along with her fur.

As soon as she was no longer whole, the flames would sneak inside her.

Burn her up from the inside out. Kill her.

She didn't care if Dick promised Angelina that he'd stop as soon as she acquiesced.

Merilee was taking the decision out of his hands.

She'd never thought about killing herself before.

Not until now.

The claws she'd extended from her paw appeared to glitter darkly, even as the flames blackened them.

They were still strong enough to pierce. To cut. To slash at her own throat.

It was just a tiny cut. Something she might do accidentally scratching herself.

The pain of that small scrape along her throat was nothing compared to taking that flame inside of her own body. The heat extinguished all thought, all sensation, except pain.

Merilee discovered that she could howl now, her piercing shriek cutting through the smoke that surrounded her, engulfed her, burned her from the inside out.

She wailed again when she discovered she could move. She launched herself across the table, trying to land on Dick, take her with him.

To no avail.

He backhanded her, hard enough that she flew through the air and smacked her head against the conference room wall.

Merilee thought that would have been the end of it. But no.

The flames went out abruptly as she landed, wrecked, on the floor.

"Merilee! Merilee!" Angelina was crying. She came over, her hands hovering, hesitant to touch Merilee, to accidentally cause her more pain.

"Mrrow," Merilee whispered. She needed touch. She needed contact.

Angelina understood for once. She picked up her sister's broken body and placed it in her lap.

Merilee wished she could purr. Her uptight sister would never have gotten her skirt so dirty, picking up a singed and dying kitty.

This Angelina would though. The good one.

The good witch.

Who was about to go bad.

The last thing Merilee saw was Dick rubbing the back of the hand that had struck her. The flesh had turned black and had been burned.

Good.

She'd only hurt him a little.

Next time, she'd hurt him a lot.

She gave one last long kitty sigh, then let go of the pain, the anguish, and this life.

～

Strange. Though Merilee awoke alone in the conference room, she felt as though someone else was there.

It wasn't someone icky, like Dick the Elf. No, this was a comforting presence.

"Mrrow?" Merilee said, the sound coming out faint and hollow.

She couldn't say for certain, but it felt as though Angelina was still there, still caring for her, looking out for her.

"Mrrow," Merilee said, this time assuring Angelina that she was on her way back.

Still, she hesitated.

She was about to embark on her last life. There would be no turning back after this. No returning to the world. This was it.

They had to be smarter about this next confrontation.

Fortunately, Merilee now had some ideas, particularly since she'd finally met Dick the Elf.

Sniggering to herself, Merilee calmly walked into the portal.

Crap.

It was much worse going through it this time. The worst it had ever been. She was both burning up as well as freezing. Hard pellets rained down on already bruised and burned skin. Her eyes wept blood and her claws cracked and splintered, sending streaks of additional pain through her paws.

Her soul felt like a ten-pound anchor behind her, that she was having to drag along with her. Normally, it wouldn't have been that much of a weight. But as she was barely ten pounds herself, it was onerous. Uphill, in the snow, both directions.

Eventually, Merilee made it out the other side of the

portal. She had to step carefully, or the calming light would have whisked her away.

No, she was determined to return. To try, one last time.

Somehow, she and Angelina had to make it work. Come up with a good, effective plan.

Or else all these lives, all this pain, would have been for nothing.

Determined, Merilee turned her face away from the light, heading into the uncertainty of life one last time.

LIFE NINE

Merilee came back to life with a start. One moment, she had been dreaming, floating in between the planes of existence.

The next, she was taking a deep breath, smelling her sister's sorrow, the lingering scent of smoke, the awful taste of burning flesh still at the back of her throat.

"Mrrow?" Merilee asked as she stretched a little.

She was lying on her sister's lap. Her long white fur had mostly recovered, but it was patchy at best. Her voice sounded rough, as hoarse as if she'd been yelling at someone all day.

All her joints ached. She knew that the next time she ate anything, even food that Angelina had cut up and put through a grinder, she'd lose more teeth. She no longer had all her claws, either front or back. Her neck hurt from where she'd scratched herself, a wound that went soul deep.

"You came back," Angelina said, wonder in her voice. "I wasn't sure if you would or not. I knew you had at least one more life. But it's always so hard on you to cross over."

"Mrrow," Merilee said. She gave a soft sigh and collapsed further into Angelina's lap.

Her sister moved soothing fingers across her fur, scritching just right along her jaw. Merilee closed her eyes in sheer bliss for a few moments, her purr motor engaging with rumbles she both felt as well as heard.

"Yup, you're louder again," Angelina said.

Merilee could hear the smile in her voice. As well as the catch in her throat.

"You're so thin," her sister continued. "Just skin and bones. You've shrunk. You look so frail."

"Mrrow," Merilee insisted. Angelina would soon find out just how tough her younger sister was. As soon as she had a good long nap.

"I'm not risking you. Not ever again," Angelina said. "Besides, what would Mom say if I lost you? She'd never forgive me. And I'd never forgive myself."

Merilee didn't like where this was going. She shook herself, and forced herself up to standing.

Whoa. She wasn't quite stable yet on her feet.

"See what I mean?" Angelina said. "You're already so old. The least I can do it to take care of you for the rest of your days."

Merilee narrowed her eyes and peered sharply at Angelina. Then she glanced around the conference room.

They were alone. Where had Dick the Elf gone?

"Don't worry, you're safe," Angelina said.

Merilee wasn't actually that concerned with her safety.

"Mrrow?" she inquired. *And you?*

"I'm fine," Angelina said, trying to brush off Merilee's concerns. "I wasn't the one who just died, remember?"

Merilee shook her head. No, her sister hadn't had to die.

She'd just had to watch someone she loved take her own life.

Merilee walked forward, placing two paws on Angelina's thigh and looked up at her.

Agreement?

"What do you mean, agreement?" Angelina asked.

The way she looked to the side told Merilee almost everything she needed to know.

"Mrrowww!" Merilee said.

Angelina nodded. "Okay, yes. I had to come to an agreement with Dick. Or he would have killed you. Again. And I would have lost you forever."

Merilee had figured that much out for herself. What were the terms?

"I continue to work for him. Same deal as before. I will be making some nice money, Merilee. Really nice money. Enough to keep you in kibble for life," she said, starting to sound defensive.

Merilee just rolled her eyes at Angelina. "Mrrow?"

"And? And what?" Angelina seemed honestly confused.

Merilee stared hard at Angelina, forcing the words up one at a time.

And how are we going to stop him?

"Stop him? We can't, little sister," Angelina said with a bitter laugh. "We lost. He won."

Merilee refused to believe that. Refused to just let Angelina give up, give in to the darker magic.

There was still good in her sister. She'd seen it. Had watched Angelina start to blossom again, away from that black tide.

Merilee wasn't about to give up.

Really, Angelina should know better than to try to out-stubborn a cat.

However, Merilee didn't say anything else. Rather, she allowed Angelina to pick her up, hold her as she made her way to the door.

Just before they left, Merilee saw something.

She suddenly wiggled in Angelina's arms, her claws out.

"Ow!" Angelina said, dropping Merilee.

Uffff. She shouldn't do that unless she was prepared. Landing awkwardly wasn't good for her hips.

But Merilee didn't complain. Much. Instead, she hopped back up on the table.

Dick had left that cat-to-human amulet there.

She headed straight for it, then sat down. Looked at it, then back up at Angelina, who was still looking at the long scratch she had on her arm from Merilee.

Finally, Angelina noticed where Merilee was sitting.

"I see," she said, sounding pissed. She scooped up the amulet with one hand, putting it into one of the pockets of her skirt. Then picked up Merilee with the other.

Sue was standing just outside.

"Now, you know that there's a strict 'no pet' policy here at the office," she said gloatingly, as if anticipating the punishment she was about to mete out.

"I know," Angelina said. She sounded tired all of a sudden.

Wait. This was the Sue who'd known about magic, right? Who wasn't magical herself?

No, she wasn't magical. She was a minion. One of Dick's.

Strange. Merilee would have thought that Angelina would be furious at being betrayed by a supposed friend like Sue.

That was all right.

Merilee could be angry for her.

As well as get her revenge.

With a loud demanding yowl, Merilee twisted in Angelina's grasp, scratching her again in the process.

"Damn it!" Angelina said as she dropped Merilee.

At least this time, Merilee properly positioned herself and landed easily on her own four feet.

Then she raced off.

"What? Where is she going?" Sue demanded, as she chased after Merilee, Angelina in tow.

Merilee snickered to herself.

Oh, Sue. You picked the wrong sisters to piss off.

It was easy to trace Sue's scent back to her desk. Even easier to hop up onto her desk, spill her coffee across her keyboard and smash her monitor down on the floor.

Oopsie.

When Angelina made to grab for her again, Merilee jumped down, under the desk.

Supposedly hiding. Cowering even.

"Come back here!" Angelina said sternly.

Good. Her sister was making a lot of noise, calling for her. Maybe it would cover the sound of Merilee hacking up a large hairball.

Right under Sue's desk.

"Ewww," Angelina said, backing away quickly.

Merilee followed her handiwork with a quick, short piss.

Then she sauntered out from underneath the desk as if she'd done nothing wrong and butter wouldn't melt in her mouth. No, really, you can just leave all that cream right there. She wouldn't touch a drop!

Angelina scooped her up with angry hands. Merilee complained, but didn't try to wriggle out again.

The smell of what Merilee had accomplished made itself known through the entire office.

"What are you feeding that feline?" Sue asked. She was actually holding her nose. Good.

"I have no idea what got into her," Angelina said.

Merilee could hear the smugness in her sister's tone.

Sue had just gotten a taste of what was coming to her.

"You know, I don't care much for your attitude," Sue steamed.

"You know, I don't care much for yours, either," Angelina said. "I'm resigning. Effective two weeks from today. However, I'm taking the two weeks of paid vacation that I'm owed and leaving now."

Angelina spun on her heel and marched over to her office.

"Can you be good? At least for five minutes?" she asked Merilee quietly.

Merilee just rolled her eyes. She wasn't that much of an asshole.

She wouldn't attack anyone else in the office. Not unless Angelina pointed them out as someone worthy of Merilee's attention.

Instead, Merilee curled up on the desk, her tail wrapped snuggly around her body, waiting while Angelina took more like ten minutes to clear out everything in her desk that was of a personal nature.

As much as Angelina might have complained about living at the office sometimes, she had actually kept very little here that she couldn't just walk away from.

Merilee sat on top of the box Angelina carried out the door, the backpack stuffed with heavier books. Only a couple of people seemed sad that Angelina was on her way, including one incredibly cute guy who kind of looked like an accountant, complete with the blue shirt with white stripes and the geeky suspenders.

The rest of the office, though, looked pleased to be getting rid of the Mighty Angelina.

It wasn't their fault. They just hadn't known the real person, underneath all the hardassness.

Angelina maintained a good front, down the elevator and out to the parking lot, dumping the box (and Merilee) into the backseat, before finally collapsing as she sank into the driver's seat.

"Oh, Merilee, what have I done?" she asked fretfully.

"Mrrow," Merilee assured her. It was going to be all right.

They would fix this Dick. Then they'd fix the rest of Angelina's life.

And possibly Merilee's as well.

CHAPTER 37

When they got back to the house, Angelina fixed herself a nice hot cup of instant chicken soup, despite the fact that it was the middle of May and rather warm out. Merilee had what remained of the chicken breast from earlier. Then the pair of them went into the back yard.

Angelina's lawn chairs were still folded up in the garden shed from the winter. Angelina got out two and dragged them across, setting them up at the bottom of the hill. She performed the "speak with animals" spell on herself so that she and Merilee could communicate better.

But before they started talking, they both sat blissfully in the sunshine, soaking up the beams.

"You know, I always felt guilty taking Mondays off," Angelina murmured after a while. "Today, I just don't care. Maybe I should, but I can't."

"Money?" Merilee asked.

"I've got enough," Angelina said. She laughed quietly to herself, both of them reflecting on her accusations of Dick. "I really do. I can last for a few months on my own, without the high-paying job. Then things are going to get a lot tighter. Particularly since I have another mouth to feed."

Merilee just shook her head. She could always go hunting for her food.

Mind you, it would be more difficult, given her age. But she could still do it. And she wouldn't complain too much. Probably.

"Which is why working for Dick is more important than ever," she said after a few moments. "I just don't see how I'm going to get out of this."

Merilee sighed softly, not putting much effort into it. She'd only rate herself a four or five, honestly, on the scale of kitty sighs.

"I would like to try something, though," Angelina said, reaching her hand into her pocket and pulling out the amulet.

She leaned over and placed it on Merilee's chair.

Merilee sniffed at it. Though her sense of smell wasn't as acute as it had been just a few days ago, she could still tell that there wasn't any bad magic contained in the amulet. It was what it claimed to be. A spell for transforming someone or something into a human.

Because it was the amulet making the transformation, and not Merilee, it would get around the "humans only have one life" thing. She'd still be a cat on the inside. She'd just appear as a human.

Something was bothering her, though. She nosed at the amulet, flipping it over onto the other side. It had a single character carved into the center of it, a symbol that even she could read. "One."

One what? One day, perhaps? One hour? One week?

Finally, it all came together for Merilee.

"Short span," she said. She pushed at the amulet. "Wood. Not metal."

Angelina picked up the amulet, feeling it between her fingers. "You're right. The spells are thin. It can change you into a human, but the transformation wouldn't last."

Merilee sat back as Angelina's temper came to the forefront.

"Damn him! It's another way of hooking us, isn't it? If I want you to be human, I'm going to have to keep working for him, so he can keep giving me amulets," she snapped.

Merilee nodded. That was all true.

"You learn spells?" she asked, indicating the amulet that Angelina still held.

"What, can I learn these spells? Make you another amulet? I'm…I'm not sure," Angelina said after a few moments.

She studied the round piece in her hand. "Maybe," she said slowly. "It would take time. Time we don't have. Richard—Dick—already got me to agree to some work." A sad cloud crossed Angelina's face. "And I'm going to have to start using the dark magic again."

Merilee chirped and patted the lawn chair.

Angelina leaned over and put the amulet back down in front of her.

"We need to come up with a plan to defeat him," Angelina complained, leaning back in her chair and contemplating the bright blue sky up above. "At first, the dark magic was kind of sexy, you know? It didn't feel bad. Now, the thought of going back to it, it's like going for a dip in a polluted lake. That slime is going to be everywhere, and will eventually start crawling under my skin."

That actually heartened Merilee. The longer Angelina stayed clean, working as a good witch, the better she was going to be able to resist the temptation to backslide.

Merilee didn't doubt that lure would always be there. She

knew that there would be times when Angelina would long for all that power again.

The ability to call up lightning again.

Lightning.

That caught Merilee's attention. She could never have done such a thing. She'd never had the power.

But Angelina had.

She looked back at the amulet sitting so innocently between her paws as a plan formed.

Either it would work.

Or possibly they'd have to find each other somewhere else —either in Heaven or in Hell.

CHAPTER 38

It took a full week of preparation, of casting spells and enchanting items. Angelina complained bitterly about the cost more than once. Merilee got her to stop grousing with a look every time.

Enough. They would have enough if this all worked out.

Merilee tried to get used to the collar that Angelina bought for her. It was a pretty white collar with what looked like fake diamond studs in it, each about the diameter of a penny. It went well with both her white fur as well as her black fur. (She tended to wear her white fur mostly, now. It was easier to hide how patchy her coat had gotten. Plus, it was also easier to ensure that all of Angelina's pristine furniture was now properly covered in cat fur.)

She didn't like the collar. The first couple of times she'd slept in it, she woken up with nightmares that she was choking. And she hated the dangling tags from it. It had taken a lot of work to learn how to move silently, so that they didn't clang, even if one was made of wood.

But if Angelina could get used to the things she was

doing that week, Merilee was just going to have to suck it up as well.

The most fun part of the whole week was doing magic together.

Human magic had to be learned, taught, handed down from one generation to the next. There was some level of experimenting that particularly strong witches might do, tweaking this spell or that.

Cat magic, on the other hand, was intuitive, instinctual, and had to be figured out. Merilee had the feeling that even if she'd been born a cat, she wouldn't have learned much from her mom or siblings. Cat magic was much more individualistic, depending on the cat.

And she wasn't just being egotistic. Angelina agreed.

"It's why every witch's familiar can do different things," she explained one evening as they sat in the kitchen nook, taking a short break. Merilee's water dish had a permanent place on the table, now. Angelina sat stirring the peppermint tea in front of her, not drinking. She wore more comfortable clothes all the time. Merilee knew that her sister had already contemplated burning all of her work gear.

They would have to cross that path later.

The night settled in around them, cozy and warm. The day had been a success, at least in terms of their preparation.

They had one more spell to do together before the next day, when Dick wanted Angelina to come out to his house so they could work together again.

"Mrrow?" Merilee asked.

"Tied?" Angelina replied. "What do you mean? Oh! Are a witch and her familiar tied together?"

Merilee nodded. She really didn't know that much about familiars, as she'd never had one. And she still really wasn't one, though people might mistake her for one. Particularly after the spells that they'd been doing.

"Yes, their fates are tied together," Angelina said, nodding. "Not in a bad way, though. I know that those thugs, Nialto, Bennet, and Daryl, thought that if they hurt you, they'd hurt Merilee." She paused for a moment, listening to what she'd just said. "You know what I mean. That if they hurt the cat who they thought was Merilee's familiar, they'd hurt my sister. They were right, but wrong at the same time."

Merilee tilted her head to the side. She'd learned so much about magic this past week, working with her sister.

Then again, Angelina had learned a lot too, as they'd worked together performing magic, Angelina standing stock still at the head of whatever focus circle she'd drawn, Merilee either walking around the circle or winding her way between Angelina's legs.

"While harming a familiar might temporarily stun a witch, diminish her powers, it isn't permanent. Whatever strength she gave to the familiar eventually flows back into the witch. And vice versa," Angelina added. "If a witch dies, the familiar is merely in shock for a short while. Then it goes back to its normal life. If it can."

Merilee nodded, thoughtful. It was the one thing they hadn't tried yet, to see if Merilee could become Angelina's familiar.

As Merilee had started as a human, not as a cat, she didn't think that she could be called that way. Angelina hadn't wanted to try.

It would have strengthened them both, the two of them pooling their power together to form a greater whole.

It also would have messed up the rest of their plans.

"Are we ready?" Angelina finally asked, the one question that hovered between them like morning mist. "There's just so much that can go wrong," she fretted.

"Mrrow," Merilee said softly, walking forward and butting her head against Angelina's arm.

They'd done all they could do in terms of spells and preparation. Tomorrow, they'd just have to make the best of it.

The pair of them got up from the nook together, back to the circle that took up most of the space in the grand living room floor. Candles burned on every surface. Angelina complained more than once about how much energy her cleaning spells now took to get the wax off everything.

Angelina took up her usual spot at the head of the circle, on the north. Merilee wove her way around the circle, sometimes going clockwise, other times, counterclockwise. It all depended on the spell.

Tonight, a large, pink stuffed bear sat in the center, the container that they'd eventually choosen. It was at least five feet tall seated, with wide button eyes and a surprised expression on its face.

By herself, Angelina couldn't have done half of the magic they'd accomplished this week. Neither could Merilee. But together, they had something special going.

Merilee crooned to herself as they work, weaving together the spells that Angelina cast with her own. Hers were composed of short words, whatever came to her that was appropriate. Angelina worked with a more formal structure, taking pieces of memorized spells and speaking them out loud.

The pressure inside the circle increased. Merilee's fur crackled, standing on end. The smell of rancid oil and sweet peppermint came wafting out.

The bear shrank as their spell continued, the color shifting from bright pink to lavender.

Down went the container, compacting in on itself, growing dense with purpose.

Finally, when they ended the spell, a small cat toy now sat in the center of the circle. It had a lavender, corduroy body, with green felt ears and a green tail made out of satin string.

Merilee had the strange sensation of looking at the mouse with her eyes, then for a brief moment, staring at it with her sister's eyes. The size of the mouse shrank and the colors grew more vivid.

Then the sensation passed.

Angelina broke the circle and walked over to pick up the mouse. She weighed it in her hands for a moment, before tossing it over to Merilee.

Merilee's first impulse was to bat it back at Angelina. Instead, she made herself catch it, sniffing at it.

It was heavier than it looked, stuffed full of spells and such.

Would it be enough?

They'd find out tomorrow.

Merilee tried to stay awake as they drove out to Dick the Elf's evil mansion. She couldn't help herself, though. The movement of the car made her sleepy, and the heat from the seat warmer was exquisite.

Fortunately, Angelina didn't seem to mind. She drove them smoothly, or at least Merilee didn't wake up due to her sister taking any crazy curves or braking suddenly.

As soon as the car turned off, Merilee awoke. She stood and stretched immediately, arching her back to work all the kinks out, before flexing it.

It didn't feel quite as good as it once had. It was still better than any sort of stretching she'd ever done as a human.

Angelina sat staring out the windshield, her eyes unfocused. "He's increased the protection spells around the building," she said slowly.

While Dick didn't have the necessary strength to do all the magic he wanted, he had several other witches who acted as his minions, casting spells for him. His primary strength was still in foresight.

Hopefully, he'd never see this coming.

"Mrrow?" Merilee inquired.

"No, I don't think I'll ever be ready," Angelina said. "I haven't faced as many deaths as you have, to be so sanguine about it."

Merilee twitched her tail, shrugging. They'd done everything they could think of to take care of that, if it happened. All of Merilee's belongings had been given away. All of her bank accounts were now in Angelina's care. Angelina's will was up to date with special letters to their mom if the worst occurred.

She'd even included a few choice paragraphs about getting revenge, if the worst occurred.

They'd done what they could. Now, they needed luck as much as anything else.

"Mrrow," Merilee said with as much confidence as she could muster.

Really. It was all going to be fine.

Angelina gave her a brave smile. "Let's go see Dick, shall we?"

She pulled the backpack out of the back seat, then held it open for Merilee to crawl into. She'd changed the fabric out again, so that the entire back was transparent and Merilee could see out, watch behind them.

The air around Dick's mansion was cool. The smell of the Mississippi River underlaid everything else. Wind blew through the nearby pines. Dusk was on its way, the sky turning lovely shades of orange and pink.

They had parked inside a small courtyard. Tall brick walls surrounded them, hard and uninviting. Even a magical cat would have difficulty scaling them. Two other cars were parked nearby. Merilee caught the scent of Sue, as well as a stranger.

Great. The gang was all here.

Angelina paused for a moment, taking one last deep breath, before she walked toward the door.

Dick must have been standing there, as Merilee didn't hear the door open.

"Greetings, young one!" he said jovially.

Merilee was afraid she'd hurt something rolling her eyes.

"I'm so glad you've decided to rejoin our little family. Oh! And you've brought your sister, too! She's really going to enjoy this evening," Dick continued.

There was a surprisingly small amount of dust in the air. Old Dick's cleaning spells did a better job down here than up in the tower.

The rank odor of his magic still spread over everything, like a thin coat of tainted oil that you could never quite scrub off.

The door that shut behind them was solid oak. Interesting how magical bars flung themselves across it, now that they were safely inside.

Those bars, unfortunately, would be effective both against people coming in as well as trying to leave.

The hallways itself wasn't very well lit. All Merilee had was the impression of dark wood and closed-in spaces. Shelves with books and gross knickknacks like baseballs and trophies.

Eventually, they walked into a more open area, that actually had some light in it. Merilee smelled the presence of other people

"You already know Sue, right?" Dick said. "I know you had a little confrontation earlier. I need for you to get over that, though, and continue to work together."

"I quit," Angelina said. "I'm not going back there to work."

"Fine by me, but you'll be working together here, you

know," Dick explained. "And this fine young man is Chester."

Merilee could smell his too greasy hair from where she was seated. His magic stank of rotten rosewater and those obnoxious "manly-men" body sprays. Ugh. He was a mama's boy who'd been turned away from his mother, probably corrupted by Dick.

Angelina walked forward. Given the wince she gave, Chester must have tried to break her fingers with his "firm" handshake.

Merilee kept her growl to herself, but really, Chester, there were better ways to impress a woman.

"These two are going to monitor everything we do tonight," Dick continued.

"You don't trust me?" Angelina said.

Merilee liked the smile she heard in her sister's voice.

"No, I don't, quite frankly," Dick replied.

Huh. Merilee was surprised that he'd be honest about, well, anything.

"You walked away from me," Dick said. "And I know you didn't come back fully willingly. So whatever little spells you have planned, or games you want to play, I want you to forget all about them. They aren't going to work. Not on me. Not tonight."

"I wouldn't plan anything," Angelina said hotly.

"No? You've been planning all week," Dick replied. "You stink of magic. Your plans won't work. You forget, I'm a Seer. Though I tend to focus on natural events, that doesn't mean I didn't spend a lot of time forecasting this evening."

Merilee nearly purred. Good. They'd been planning on that.

They hadn't necessarily been planning on the other two being present. Angelina did have a couple of backup spells handy, just in case someone came running in to save Dick from his inevitable fate.

They'd just end up using those sooner rather than later.

"We should get started then, shouldn't we?" Angelina said with a hint of impatience.

Merilee found it interesting that Dick took a long pause before speaking.

"Leave the backpack here," he instructed.

Luckily, they'd anticipated that.

"What, so you can cat-nap her? Hold her hostage? Continue to use her against me? No. Merilee comes with me. She'll be safer that way," Angelina said stubbornly.

"She stays in a containment field of my making," Dick the Elf insisted.

Also good.

Things were going according to plan.

Which just meant that the really big screwup was going to happen soon.

CHAPTER 40

The casting room was in the basement of the house, dug straight into the bluffs. Plain gray cinderblocks made up the walls. A round candelabra hung in the center of the space, decorated with moose antlers and barbed wire, a disturbing combination. The casting circle in the center had been burned into the cement floor, probably with acid. There was no way to disturb that circle, or break it.

It had taken a lot of magic to create this place. Merilee was almost impressed.

Almost, until she smelled the death that lingered in the air.

True to his core, Dick the Elf had completely drained people, other witches, of their power in order to create this space.

Never enough.

Merilee was finally let out of the backpack. She made a show of stretching herself out, working out those kinks in her back, making them all pause and look at her.

Sure, she wasn't as magnificent as she'd once been. She was still a remarkable specimen, particularly for a cat.

She didn't do more than glare at Sue and hiss once in her direction, giggling when the woman flinched.

Good. She should be scared of what Merilee could do, given free rein.

Chester's looks didn't surprise her. He was still a pimple-faced boy, though maybe he'd classify as a man-child, as he was probably in his late twenties. His round face and unfortunate skin spoke of too much sugar and not enough exercise. Greasy black hair hung down over his eyes. It was probably intended to make him look like a bad boy, but instead, he looked like a pathetic loser. The black T-shirt and pants he wore were too tight, and encased his body like the thin skin of a particularly gross slug.

Would he get skinnier as Dick used him up? Or was Dick robbing him of all his vitality, so that soon he'd collapse in a pile of his own blubber?

Finally, Merilee looked over at Angelina and nodded. She was ready.

Dick's magic was cold at first, surrounding her in a chilly magical bubble. It heated up as he went along, weaving more spells into it.

Merilee tried not to be impressed, but honestly, it was better work than she'd expected from him.

Then again, he was a Seer. He'd probably known that Merilee would be bringing her cat with her, and had prepared accordingly.

When Dick finished, he turned to Merilee and asked, "Is she your familiar? You seem very tied together."

Angelina grimaced. "No, she's not a familiar. It's much worse. She's my sister."

Dick the Elf seemed puzzled by that. Then again, he'd probably been an only child, spoiled rotten by his long-departed Mama.

Merilee tilted her head to one side as the pair of them

started preparing for that evening's casting. It was interesting to see how humans at this level worked together. Sue stayed off to one side, oozing resentment. She was merely a minion, after all. An important one, true. But she'd eventually outlive her usefulness.

Chester also didn't do much but stand there, occasionally providing power to Dick. Seemed that some of that fat stored magical energy. He was a type of battery.

Could Angelina use him as a power source? That would be kind of cool, to turn him against Dick. Though they didn't have any spells prepared for that.

Across the back of the room, a long, narrow board lit up. It was a stock counter, with three-letter combinations and prices flowing across it.

Angelina had explained that the stock symbols would flow randomly across the board. Once she started her prognostication, the stocks that had more importance, that is, the ones whose price was about to rise, would start appearing more frequently. There was one time when the entire board filled with just one stock. They'd made a lot of money that night.

It was Sue's role to watch the flow of companies, pick out not merely the most obvious winners of the night but the runners-up as well. She stood with a pencil and paper at hand, ready to take notes.

Must really frost her to be demoted to the place of mere scribe. Then again, she knew the companies that those three-letter symbols represented. She'd have a better idea of what they were getting themselves into than most.

Finally, they were ready.

Merilee could tell that all the spells so far had been fairly clean, not really tainted. It wasn't until they started reaching further into the future that it was going to get icky.

Angelina hesitated.

"It's all right," Dick assured her. "See? Nothing bad has happened before now. Nothing bad is going to happen. You're so good at this! It'll be fun. Like it used to be."

Angelina shook her head. "I'm not sure about this."

"Well, you better get sure, little lady," Dick said, still assuming that "aw shucks" routine of his was going to work.

"No, I don't think so," Angelina said. She turned to Dick, her hands raised, filled with an offensive spell.

"Now, see? Why'd you have to go and spoil all this good fun?" Dick said. He sounded so disappointed in her.

Merilee could tell that the act was partly a spell, subtly influencing all of their actions.

Luckily, she was a cat. She honestly didn't care about whatever he wanted.

Angelina kept Dick's attention on her. She'd positioned herself so that Dick the Elf's back was to Merilee.

She flung the first spell in his face.

He had the temerity to laugh at her. "Now, I knew you were going to do that."

Angelina, clearly frustrated, threw a second spell at him.

Again, it dissipated on either side of him, like a river running around a solid rock stuck in the center of it.

"And that too," Dick said, still far too full of his charming self. "Why don't you try something unexpected?"

"Like this?" Angelina said, reaching over and slugging Sue.

Merilee couldn't contain her giggles as Sue went down like a sack of wet cement.

"Now, that wasn't very nice," Dick admonished her.

But he hadn't foreseen it. Merilee felt certain of that.

Good. All they'd really needed to do was to break the script once. It would never get back on track. Hopefully they'd reached that spot sooner than Dick was prepared for.

Merilee sat back, balanced on her rear paws. With her

front paws, she grasped one of the two items that dangled from it.

The wooden one. With the funny markings on it.

Merilee concentrated on the amulet, sending her magical senses both through and around it.

It was easy to see how it worked. Normally, all she would have had to do was to step on it.

Holding it between her paws activated it just as well.

Merilee felt herself start to grow. It startled her how fast she shot up. Color sprang back into the world again, as her sense of smell faded. She balanced upright, awkward for a bit until her knees unhinged then rehinged again, going forward instead of backwards.

It was strange, supporting herself on two feet instead of four.

The collar had grown with her as they'd planned, and still circled her neck.

It took a few more moments before the transformation was complete, and Merilee stood as a human again, ready to take on the world.

CHAPTER 41

Angelina continued to throw spells at Dick the Elf, preventing him from realizing just how much had changed in the last few moments.

How he now had a much more formidable enemy at his back.

Merilee tested the boundaries of the circle that was encasing her. Yup. Same spells Angelina had used. If any living thing (human or feline, it didn't matter) stepped out of the circle, they'd die.

All part of the plan.

As they'd both speculated, Dick had been introduced to Merilee as a cat, and had continued to think of her as a cat.

He hadn't anticipated her becoming human. Hadn't foreseen it either. Had probably assumed that she would greedily consume the amulet the first chance she'd gotten, then been disappointed in how short it lasted.

Angelina and Merilee didn't think that Dick couldn't counter cat spells. However, they'd also assume that Merilee wouldn't have the space to pace in order to activate them.

What Merilee did have was a whole set of amulets, woven into her collar, created by the Almighty Angelina.

Who, at the end of the day, was still one of the strongest witches around.

Merilee pried off one of the small studs from her collar and threw it at Dick.

The crackling effect of the lightning was just too good as it zapped him in the butt.

"Whoa!" Dick complained, stepping to the side. He glanced back at her. "I don't know what kind of kink you're into, but I'm not looking for a threesome," he smirked.

It took Merilee a moment to realize what he was implying.

Of course, she was nude. Why would she be wearing clothes?

She glanced down at her skin. Olive-toned was what they called it. Not the bright pink-white of Dick's skin, but a darker, warmer color. Her body was a little thicker than she remembered it being. It was as if she'd grown more solid as a cat. She no longer had claws, but her nails were all sharp and pointed, done with a natural French manicure, the tips white.

Since she was nude, that automatically meant that she wanted to have sex with him? And her sister as well?

Where did men come up with this sort of ridiculousness?

"Though if you two wanted to go at it, I'd be happy to watch," he continued with a leer.

Angelina struck him with a particularly strong bout of magic that time, a hard push that made him shake his head.

"Now, young lady, you're going to make me angry, soon," he said. "Let's stop playing around and get down to business, shall we?" He gestured toward the waiting conjuring circle, the board of business symbols still scrolling beyond it.

Angelina threw yet another strong shove of magic his way.

Dick gave an exasperated sigh. Merilee would have given it a seven on the kitty scale.

"Don't say I didn't warn you," Dick said. He drew up his hands, seemingly reluctant, before he sent out a stream of lightning at Angelina.

Fortunately, Angelina had anticipated that would be one of his first moves, and had already set up a shield for herself.

What the fool hadn't thought about was that he was no longer facing just one witch.

He had two.

As he blasted at Angelina, Merilee threw another stud from her collar at him. The small detonation that went off at his feet deafened her for a moment.

He looked shaken, glancing back.

He really hadn't anticipated that they might attack him physically, not just magically.

Fool.

Dick narrowed his eyes as he stared at Merilee. However, before he could do anything, Angelina whacked him again with a jolting whip of magic that lashed his legs, tearing his fine pants.

Ah, such a shame! Those nice clothes, ruined!

Dick appeared to catch a clue, finally. "Chester, grab her," he said, indicating Angelina. "While I finish off the sister."

He turned resolutely toward Merilee, who sneered at him.

Pretty much anything he threw at her would kill his protective circle. Then she'd be on him.

And they'd settle this, once and for good.

Chester reached for Angelina like the greedy baby he was. However, Merilee couldn't pay attention to him, or to her sister for that matter.

Not when she was facing the Grandest Baby of them all.

"You know, we could have done some beautiful magic together, the three of us," Dick said conversationally as he started pouring magic into the protective circle.

Huh. It appeared he was trying to keep her contained.

But he'd contained a cat, originally. Not a human. Even his magical preparation wouldn't have stretched that far, or his foresight gone to that conclusion.

When flames suddenly leaped up all around her, Merilee understood. Dick wasn't going to kill her himself. He just needed for her to step out of the circle. It would do all the work for him.

Good thing Angelina had prepared for that.

Merilee tugged at the other amulet hanging from her collar. The shield effectively worked against both flames as well as ice.

She smirked at him as the flames danced all around her, her skin unharmed, the pain held at bay.

Unfortunately, Dick didn't look impressed. He was starting to look pissed off.

Merilee's smirk grew wider when she threw another stud at him and he leaped back.

A plant sprang up, flinging itself toward Dick, who was now fighting a large set of thorny vines.

Merilee had come up with that one and was rather proud of herself.

It wouldn't last long against him. Nothing would.

Dick blasted it with fire, burning the greenery into ashes.

Too bad. A few plants would really liven up this underground lair. Maybe even some catnip.

Before Dick could recover, Merilee flung another stud at him. This one didn't do anything but hit the ground and start to expand, filling rapidly like a water balloon. It was a pretty lilac color, and grew to about the size of a one-foot square cube.

Obviously, Dick had never seen anything like it before. He touched the cube gingerly with the toe of one of his loafers. It jiggled in response.

"What the—" He never got the finally word out before the cube exploded outward.

The stench was enough to bring tears to Merilee's eyes, and she was somewhat shielded from it.

Poor Dick, Chester, and even Sue were reduced to being doubled over, choking and gasping, tears streaming from their eyes.

Angelina quickly took care of Chester, dropping him to the floor. Sue, too.

She didn't close on Dick quickly enough, though. He drew a hand across his face, wiping the (okay, admittedly gross) lilac goo off and flinging it toward the floor.

"I have had enough of the pair of you," Dick raged.

Finally, he'd dropped that "good ol' boy" routine. He still kind of sounded like that actor, William H. Macy. Only now, it was Macy playing a serial killer.

The chandelier hanging from the ceiling suddenly swung to the side. It dropped without warning on Angelina. Since it was made up primarily of a circle around the bottom of it, the chandelier landed on the floor, with Angelina standing inside of it. The barbed wire "decoration" wrapped around the piece sprang up and wrapped around Angelina, tying her arms to her sides.

She was trapped.

It was all up to Merilee, now.

"You didn't really think that you were going to win, now, did you?" Dick the Elf said, sounding jovial again. "I always win."

Merilee smirked at him, and threw one last stud from her collar.

This one turned into a large net, meant to entangle the asshole.

All she needed was for his attention to be turned elsewhere for a few moments.

And for a little bit of luck.

While Dick was fighting his way out of the net, Merilee took one deep breath, then another.

It had been nice being a human, even if it had only been for a short while.

She stepped across the protection circle.

Dick grinned at Merilee as she suddenly stooped over.

Damn it! Dying as a human was going to be hard. She forced herself to focus, to count out the agonizing seconds. It didn't take any pretending to be suffering, flailing.

Her human self had to die, after all. And she had to keep all of Dick's attention on her.

What Dick wasn't counting on was that Merilee was, at heart, a cat.

Just as he was freeing himself from the last of the sticky net, Merilee felt the last of the human part of her passing away. She focused in on herself, compressing herself down, changing her bones around, her teeth, her eyes and her ears.

Blessed fur sprouted all across her back. Her leg bones rearranged themselves again. Color seeped out of the world and smell sprang back in.

Oh, it was heavenly to be back in her real body again! It felt so good! She felt as though she could leap to the top of the tower in a single bound.

Had it felt this good the first time she'd transformed? Or had she been too scared?

Merilee hissed at Dick and successfully slid to the side when he grabbed at her.

Foolish human.

She raced over to where Angelina had casually dropped the backpack, digging into it with a flurry of paws.

There it was. At the bottom of the compartment she sat in.

The mouse toy.

She dragged it out, letting it dangle happily from her mouth, as if it was a prized possession.

Dick at least had the good grace to pause when he saw her like that.

Even he could smell the magic it contained. Not necessarily the actual smells—a human nose wasn't that good.

He could still sense that there was a lot of magic packed into such a small toy.

"Okay, I don't know what that is, but you need to put it down," he said.

Aw, was the poor man worried?

Merilee made a feint forward, as if she was going to race toward him.

He jerked back.

Merilee snickered.

Dick sighed and rolled his eyes toward the ceiling. "I can't believe I'm actually going to say this," he muttered. "Here kitty, kitty, kitty."

Oh, that was too good! Merilee wished they had a recording of the great Dick the Elf calling to a mere cat.

She felt the enchantment tugging at her fur. His words had power. More than she was expecting, honestly.

One paw dragged forward, followed by another.

Damn it! She had to fight him. Had to get him to take the mouse!

"Here, kitty, kitty, kitty."

Those words drummed into her skull, reverberating through her bones. She *had* to answer the call.

Where was Angelina? No, she couldn't look at her sister. Couldn't hope for her to get free.

It was all up to Merilee, and she was failing.

Dick hadn't taken the prize yet, hadn't jerked it away from her.

"Come here, kitty. Here."

With her head down and her shoulders slouched, Merilee continued to take one heavy step after another toward Dick. It was inevitable, her walk of shame across the cold concrete, the smell of her sister's tears in the air, the smirk that Dick the Elf wore.

After all, he always won, right?

Merilee tried to stop her slow progress, her hindlegs shaking as she did. But she couldn't. She had to go to him. Had to go to that voice.

Had to make it right, for whatever version of *right* that voice demanded.

One step. Then another.

"Now, put down the mouse," the voice commanded.

Merilee considered for a moment.

There really was only so much you could ask of a cat. Even a highly trained one would rebel after a while.

That was just the nature of cats.

Something that Dick had no appreciation for.

Merilee sat back for a moment, putting her butt on the cold concrete, her tail wrapped neatly across her front paws, the mouse still dangling from her mouth like the best game ever.

"Come here and drop the mouse," Dick said.

Was the poor man losing it? Could he no longer just demand obedience from his minions?

Or had he no idea of how to deal with a cat? A cat who might, possibly, accede to one demand.

But not two. And certainly not at the same time.

"Mrrow!" Merilee said, refusing.

Dick gave an expressive sigh. Really, he was kind of good at that. Maybe a six point five on the kitty scale.

"I said drop it." That voice reverberated through the room again.

Merilee considered his request for a moment.

She paused for too long, though.

He'd successfully managed to distract her.

Rough hands scooped her up, wrapping around her belly.

Merilee automatically attacked with sharp claws, batting at the hands, the arms, the body, anything she could connect with.

She kept from yowling her displeasure, though, and didn't drop her prize.

She felt herself being lifted up. Everything was suddenly moving in slow motion.

She suddenly knew what was going to happen. Dick was going to throw her. Hard. Against a wall.

She'd probably break something. Maybe something fatal.

And she still hadn't gotten him to take the damned mouse yet.

Both she and Angelina were going to fail. They were both going to die.

And for what?

CHAPTER 43

"Put her down. Now."

Angelina's voice sounded strained, as if she was pushing against a great weight.

However, it was enough to get Dick to pause. Merilee still hung in his hands, over his head.

"Or what?" Dick had to smirk.

He thought he was the king of smirk. That he had the upper hand.

That was going to be his downfall.

"She isn't just my sister, you know," Angelina said. "She's me."

"You know, I've heard that sort of metaphysical crap all my life. What does that even mean?" Dick asked.

"Let me show you."

Perspective changed abruptly. There was no gradual shift.

Merilee suddenly saw the picture she made from her sister's eyes.

Her sister, who was all the way across the room.

Dick the Elf, that towering fool, stood with his mouth

gaping. He still had his hands wrapped in a death grip around a tiny cat body.

Then that cat body began to shift and elongate. Turn back into human.

Not back into Merilee, no.

Into Angelina.

The barbed wire that held the human body collapsed in on itself as the being it held transformed into a much smaller cat.

Merilee neatly hopped out of the reach of the chandelier while Dick struggled to hold up the full-grown woman who'd just appeared in his hands.

Just for a moment.

The transformation was never complete. It didn't have to be.

Merilee was abruptly sucked back up, whirled back into the place she was supposed to be, up above Dick's head. The mouse was still in her mouth.

It didn't take but a moment now to drop it, while he was so unsettled, unable to grasp what had just happened, unable to process how quickly the sisters had changed places, then gone back.

It had taken some time, and a lot of practice.

The main point had never been for them to switch places.

Instead, it was just one more distraction.

Merilee dropped the mouse down Dick's gaping collar, so it landed somewhere on his chest.

"You *bitch*!" he screamed.

Unfortunately, that was when he flung her across the room. She twisted, trying to prepare, but it wouldn't be enough, she knew.

All that extra time she'd borrowed had finally run out.

Merilee heard the crack her spine made as she hit the

wall. She didn't yowl until she hit the floor, unable to move much else.

The spells the mouse contained were already starting to unwind. Dick just helped it along by clutching the toy that had found its way inside his shirt.

Angelina hesitated.

"MRRROWW!" Merilee insisted. *Finish him off.*

They could see to her later.

She tried to weakly move one of her paws.

Or not.

The pain made her want to vomit, but Merilee couldn't move. It was as bad as when she'd been trapped in that asshole's flames, on the conference room table, wanting to pace, to escape, but being unable to.

Despite the tears in her eyes and the heaviness of her eyelids, Merilee still was able to watch Angelina pull out the spells they'd carefully woven into the mouse. Again, the toy had just been a distraction.

The bear started growing now, all of its stuffing spilling out on the floor as Dick fought against it.

He couldn't escape its fuzzy embrace, the pink plush surrounding him as he started to shrink down.

For a moment, it was almost comical, the look of surprise on Dick's face as the bear wrapped around him, consuming him. Particularly when it was mostly finished, and Dick appeared to be more pink, stuffed bear than human.

The last part was the most difficult. Transforming Dick had never been the problem.

No, the issue had been keeping him.

Even Merilee had to admit that turning Dick into another creature would have been evil in the end if his consciousness remained. He'd be trapped forever in a body that wouldn't ever move and forever felt *wrong*.

If there was one thing that Merilee had come to realize,

being in the right external form made all the difference in the world.

So they had to steal Dick's consciousness away. Button it up so that he didn't grow restless, bored, or insane. (All right, more insane.)

They really didn't want to torture him for all eternity. Not if they wanted to remain good witches.

Instead, they had to drain away his awareness. Push it out into the pink fuzzy plush fur of the bear. That was why the toy had to be so big in the first place, so that it could absorb all of what made Dick, well, a dick.

Only after that initial transformation was in place could Angelina start the second set of spells, turning the bear back into a tiny cat toy.

Merilee might have delighted in that choice. Maybe far too much.

The first transformation would have slipped Dick's consciousness far away, so that he could never come back awake. It wouldn't kill him. No, that was also too far off the path of good.

It would just *stop* him, forever.

Merilee's last sight was that of Dick forever entrapped in a small, lavender mouse body.

She wished she could have said a proper goodbye to her sister. But maybe it was better this way, to slip away while they accomplished what they'd started out to do.

Mrrow, Merilee said silently as her eyes closed and the darkness finally took away all the pain.

～

Merilee found that she was still in that conjuring room of Dick's. Like the last time, she didn't feel as though she was completely alone here, in this place between life and death. Her sister was nearby. She could almost smell her tears.

It had been a good life. Or lives. Merilee had helped Angelina in more ways than one. Her sister would go on to lead a good life. A better life.

For a moment, Merilee regretting not being the one to live. But honestly, after that first death, she'd never been sure she wasn't living on anything other than borrowed time.

The room grew dim quickly. Merilee couldn't wait any longer, couldn't risk being trapped here.

While it might have been fun haunting this place while Dick had still been around, with him gone, it wouldn't have nearly the same appeal.

Merilee reached out and touched the gray portal. It seemed different this time. More like the first portal she'd gone through.

With a shrug, Merilee pushed on, crossing the threshold.

Cold pierced her, passing through to her bones. It wasn't as bad as previous times, though. Her soul felt buoyed up inside of her, floating with her as she went through the endless passage.

And really? It had to tug out more of her fur? Was she going to have any left by the time she reached the other side?

Peaceful light surrounded her as she stepped out of the other side, tugging her upward.

Merilee sighed. Maybe it was all for the best.

Except—the room where she'd been was still visible.

Wait.

Was that a light spot over there? A different light that she could walk toward and through?

Maybe make her way back to the land of the living?

Merilee twisted and arched her back, trying to get herself out of the grasp of the light.

It let go of her reluctantly.

Merilee landed lightly on her feet, surprised. Why wasn't she being carried away? Why was there another path back? What exactly had happened?

She wasn't sure. She just knew that she was going to have one more chance.

And she intended to take it.

With a bounding leap, Merilee passed out of this in-between place.

Smack dab into the land of the living.

LIFE TEN?

CHAPTER 44

Merilee sat perched on her pillow looking out over the living room from her couch.

All right. So in some ways, it was technically *Angelina's* house, living room, and furniture.

Merilee still considered it hers. It had her cat fur on it, after all.

Besides, Angelina had finally gotten rid of the last of the fancy beige-and-black leather pieces, and had filled the space with much more comfortable fabric furniture. It was *their* furniture, now.

Changing her living space had been one of the many things that Angelina had done over the past six months to accommodate living with Merilee. She'd also adjusted all of the protection spells so that Merilee could create portals and come and go as she pleased.

It was raining right now, so Merilee was content to stay inside. The family had been by earlier—Mom, her cousins, a few others. Though Mom had had a hard time coming to accept that her youngest was now a cat, her cousins had been much easier to win over.

But everyone had been impressed with Merilee's magical abilities now. She'd never been able to do half as much when she'd been human.

Merilee stood up and stretched, relieving every kink that her back had accumulated. She paused for a moment, licking her chest and the fine white fur that lay there, before hopping down and making her way to the kitchen.

A snack sounded good.

Here, too, Angelina had made changes. She'd finally agreed to the long red pull hanging from the front door of the fridge so that Merilee could easily open it, without magic. Angelina hadn't wanted to put it there at first, not until she realized that if Merilee had a physical way of opening the refrigerator, she was much more like to close it afterward.

Merilee still forgot sometimes, but she tried harder not to.

The lowest shelf had all the good things on it. Chicken breasts, tuna, even a couple of containers of store-bought, raw cat food.

A girl needed variety, after all.

Merilee sat at the foot of the fridge, concentrating, trying to lift one of the containers out. It took some effort but she was getting better at it, floating the food out of the fridge then down to the floor.

"You know, if you could have waited even five minutes, or come and told me, I would have gotten your food out for you," Angelina commented as she came into the kitchen. She quickly picked the container off the floor, grabbing a spoon and a bowl.

"Mrrow," Merilee said dismissively. Where was the fun in that?

She hopped easily onto the kitchen table where Angelina dished out some food into the bowl.

"So you'll never guess who I ran into today," Angelina said as Merilee was about to dip her head into her food.

Merilee glanced over her shoulder. She was interested in what Angelina had to say, of course, but...but...food was right under her nose. News could wait. She started eating.

"Chester," Angelina said, giving Merilee a few moments of peace. She chuckled. "He nearly wet himself when he saw me. Quickly went the other direction. I could tell that he isn't doing much magic these days."

Merilee merely nodded, concentrating on what was important. The food in front of her.

"You do realize that we're both safe, now. No one's coming after us for the disappearance of Dick the Elf."

Merilee stopped eating, turned away from her food dish and back toward Angelina. "Mrrow?"

"And, that means you could go back to being human, you know," Angelina said.

Merilee couldn't help but roll her eyes again, then turned back to eating.

"I know, I know," Angelina said. "But there's this new spell I've found..."

Merilee gave a heavy kitty sigh as she stopped eating again.

No one was exactly sure what had happened. The best explanation that they could come up with was that when Merilee had been transformed from a cat into human, not through the amulet but by temporarily changing places with Angelina, she'd reset her "clock" as it were.

Instead of losing her last life, she'd gone back to having nine.

Eight, probably, after the one that she'd lost at Dick's hands.

So maybe she could go back to being human. Or maybe she'd lost that human life already.

It didn't matter.

Merilee walked over to the edge of the table where Angelina was sitting, looking up at her. They weren't quite eye-to-eye, but it was close enough.

I don't want to change back.

Angelina sighed. "Are you sure? I keep wondering. Are you really happy? As a cat?"

Merilee leaned forward and butted her head against Angelina's chin. Of course, she was happy as a cat. She got to spend her day lounging and being adored. Or she could transport herself outside, play, chase butterflies or mice.

As for magic, why wouldn't she want to stay in the form where she had so much more power?

"All right," Angelina said, scritching Merilee perfectly, finding that spot along the bottom of her jowl. It had taken forever to train her. "But you let me know if you ever change your mind."

Merilee sat back and looked Angelina in the eye again. She nodded once, firmly.

Then she turned and went back to her dinner. Magic and sharing could wait until after she finished eating.

Leah Cutter writes page-turning fiction in exotic locations, such as a magical New Orleans, the ancient Orient, Hungary, the Oregon coast, rural Kentucky, Seattle, Minneapolis, and many others.

She writes literary, fantasy, mystery, science fiction, and horror fiction. Her short fiction has been published in magazines like *Alfred Hitchcock's Mystery Magazine* and *Talebones*, anthologies like Fiction River, and on the web. Her long fiction has been published both by New York publishers as well as small presses.

Find Leah's books on Knotted Road Press at (www.KnottedRoadPress.com)

Follow her blog at www.LeahCutter.com.

Reviews

It's true. Reviews help me sell more books. If you've enjoyed this story, please consider leaving a review of it on your favorite site.

Come someplace new...

Are you a traveler? Do you enjoy exploring strange new worlds, new cultures, new people?

Journey into the various lands envisioned by Leah Cutter.

Sign up for my newsletter and I'll start you on your travels with a free copy of my book, *The Island Sampler*.

I will never spam you or use your email for nefarious purposes. You can also unsubscribe at any time.

http://www.LeahCutter.com/newsletter/